KAGEROU DAZE

VOLUME 5: **THE DECEIVING**

JIN (SHIZEN NO TEKI-P)
ILLUSTRATED BY SIDU

NEW YORK

KAGEROU DAZE, Volume 5
JIN (Shizen no Teki-P)

Translation by Kevin Gifford
Cover art by SIDU

KAGEROU DAZE V -the deceiving-
©KAGEROU PROJECT/1st PLACE

First published in Japan in 2014 by KADOKAWA CORPORATION ENTERBRAIN.

English translation rights arranged with KADOKAWA CORPORATION ENTERBRAIN, through Tuttle-Mori Agency, Inc., Tokyo.

English translation © 2016 by Yen Press, LLC

Yen On
1290 Avenue of the Americas
New York, NY 10104

Visit us at yenpress.com
facebook.com/yenpress
twitter.com/yenpress
yenpress.tumblr.com

First Yen On Edition: September 2016

Yen On is an imprint of Yen Press, LLC.
The Yen On name and logo are trademarks of Yen Press, LLC.

Library of Congress Cataloging-in-Publication Data

Names: Jin, 1990– author. | SIDU, 1993– illustrator. | Gifford, Kevin, translator.
Title: Kagerou daze. Volume 5, The deceiving / JIN (Shizen no Teki-P) ;
   illustrated by SIDU ; translation by Kevin Gifford.
Other titles: Kagero deizu. English | Deceiving
Description: First Yen On edition. | New York, NY : Yen On, 2016.
Identifiers: LCCN 2016019948 | ISBN 9780316545280 (paperback)
Subjects: | CYAC: Teenagers—Japan—Fiction. | Ability—Fiction. | Criminals—Fiction. |
   BISAC: FICTION / Science Fiction / General.
Classification: LCC PZ7.1.J55 Kak 2016 | DDC [Fic]—dc23 LC record available at
   https://lccn.loc.gov/2016019948

ISBNs: 978-0-316-54528-0 (paperback)
   978-0-316-46601-1 (ebook)

10 9 8 7 6 5 4 3 2

LSC-C

Printed in the United States of America

CONTENTS

YOBANASHI DECEIVE 0

"...No, no, it's true. What reason would I have to lie about it?"

The girl looked at me dubiously in response.
She must have doubted me from the outset.

...Which would be the smart thing to do.
When you considered the ability I had to deceive people's eyes, that was the most prudent path for anyone to take.

"Don't believe me, huh...? All I'm trying to do is lead you back to your original body."
The girl stubbornly refused to nod at me.
Well, I figured as much.
Who'd say yes to such a blatantly fishy tale? Nobody. Of course not.

And I have good reason to talk like this, too.
It's not like I'm seeking to make her dislike me.
I just want people to keep wondering about me. Doubting me. Doubting someone who can't even trust himself.

I don't understand myself at all.
What do I like? What don't I like? What do I want to achieve? Why am I here?
What am I, really, on the inside? I still had no idea.
I wouldn't want anyone to believe anything a guy like that told them.
They should doubt it. Deny it. Tear it down to pieces, for all I care.
Then, from the rubble, the real me might pop its face out. I'd like to see that for myself again.

*   *   *

...Though, maybe even *that's* a lie.

Thanks to the lies piled atop lies, I've become completely unable to say what I really mean any longer. It's irritating.

However, she really is a good girl.

She's got this amazingly strong, refined sense of self. And the ability to doubt people. I'm practically jealous.

"Okay, well, how 'bout we do this? I could tell you some stories and stuff on the way there; how 'bout that? You won't get all bored that way. You're free to go if you do, though."

The girl's expression still oozed suspicion.

Yes. That'll work for me.

"I mean, it won't be weird stories or anything, right? I'll just tell you about my life and stuff. It's nothing too exciting, but at least it'll keep you occupied, y'know?"

"...Here, how 'bout I give you a little taster?"

ONE DAY, ON A ROOF

"So then, like, Haruka ate the entire thing! His doctor told him to knock it off and stuff, but he was all, like, 'Oh, it's fine, it really tastes good, so...'"

Takane paused to sigh, obviously still in a huff over it.

The breeze felt good up here, on the roof, in the early afternoon.

The concrete floor beneath us was slightly warm to the touch, under the bright midspring sun.

It had been around ten minutes since I had sat down and begun talking to Takane.

"Ha-ha-ha! He's always a handful for you, isn't he, Takane?"

Takane furrowed her brows at my innocent reply. "Ugghh, just talking about it makes me angry all over again."

She was a sophomore at this high school, part of the special-ed program.

Her favorite food was simmered yellowtail with radish. Her least favorite was tomatoes.

She was a gifted gamer, too. That served as both her regular hobby and her daily addiction.

She was an only child, living with her grandmother; her parents were apparently working overseas somewhere.

But among all of those unique personality traits, the one that always stuck out the most was how constantly irritated she was.

Even now, although her complaint was hardly anything serious, her body language indicated extreme annoyance.

If it irks her that much, why does she even have to talk about it? That was my honest take.

But I suppose it was the way she stuck to that habit that made her…more innocent—girlish, if you will—than she would've been otherwise.

There was no hiding the fact that Takane had a thing for Haruka, a guy she went to class with.

She hadn't officially declared that herself yet, but picking up on it was easy when she started nearly every conversation with "I can't *believe* what Haruka did!"

From that, I had to surmise that Takane's constant moaning was her way of expressing her affinity for the boy.

If I found myself saying something like, "Oh man, that dude Haruka's the *worst*," who knows what kind of wrath that could trigger. That was drama I didn't need in my life.

That's what I always strove for: a life without drama. One where I never got in the way of anyone.

And that was always what I had to keep in mind during conversations like these. Going to this school, it was a must.

"He's incredibly late, though, isn't he? Geez. How long does it take for someone to go out and buy lunch?"

"Well…maybe the cafeteria's really crowded or something."

"Yeah, *suuuure*," Takane snorted. She never accepted anything at face value. It was vicious.

Well, not that I have much right to judge.

As she stared at the metal door separating the roof level from the stairway leading up to it, Takane opened her mouth, as if suddenly remembering something.

"…Oh. Hey, while nobody else is around, I wanted to ask you something."

"Sure. What is it?"

"Well...um, maybe this is kinda weird, all of a sudden..."

Takane's eyes drifted into space.

What *was* it? More of her mindless complaining?

"...Is there anyone you...like, or whatever, Ayano?"

The question threw me a little. From her, it was surprising. I didn't think Takane was even sensitive to that sort of thing, really.

"Anyone I like? That's kind of sudden."

"Huh?! Oh! Is it? I mean, you don't have to say if you don't want to! Ha-ha-ha!"

Takane flailed her hands a little, her voice ratcheting up in tone.

Why was she in such a panic over my response? *This is ridiculous.*

"No, no, it's totally fine," I replied. "I don't...really have any-one, so..."

Her hands stopped in midair, and her eyes opened wide.

"Wh-what? Is it that weird to you?" I hedged.

"N-no, no..."

Takane followed that up with a distracted giggle or two. From *that* act, it was pretty clear what kind of response she wanted from me.

She probably wanted me to say that I liked *him*.

...Pondering over that depressed me a little.

I almost wanted to stand up and head home right that moment, even. Not that I could. I tried my best to change the subject.

"He *is* pretty late, though, isn't he? Hopefully he'll be back soon..."

"Oh, totally!" Takane took the bait. "What the heck is he *doing*? I'm, like, *super*-hungry!"

...How much longer do I have to wait for them to bring lunch back up for us?

Then I would have to watch every word I uttered to this girl. *What a bother...*

And *his* face, in particular. I didn't want to see it, if I could help it.

Ever since the first time I met him, in fact. Something about it just made me want to smack him.

Just then, we heard the door latch clank open.

"Hey! Sorry we're so late 'n everything! Bet you're hungry, huh?"

"Well, what do you expect? It was a madhouse down there."

Two voices boomed out from the doorway.

They were quicker than I expected, but oh well. *Just keep enjoying the day.* No roadblocks, no obstacles. No interference.

With a light breath, I gave *the brightest smile I could* and said:

"Welcome back, Shintaro."

"...Hmm. Kinda hurts a lot, actually."

My face instinctively twitched at the stinging pain.
I brought a hand to my right cheek, the source of the discomfort, only to feel a burning sensation run from my cold fingertips to the center point of my head.
I was punched sometime around eleven in the morning.
Several hours had passed since then, but the pain showed no sign of fading away. In fact, my cheek was warmer than ever and starting to swell up.

"Man, what a pain this is."
There should be a cold compress of some sort in the fridge. It came with the cake my mom had brought.
That would probably help keep the swelling down a bit.
If this left a bruise, *that* would be some serious trouble.
Last time, the women around the neighborhood pelted me with questions like, "Why are you hurt?" and "Who hit you?"
It was pure hell, really.
If a bunch of weird strangers showed up at our front door this time, too, I didn't know what I'd do.
Why can't they just mind their own business? Why do they just have to stick their necks into every stupid little thing that happens around here?
Besides, to me, this really wasn't a big deal at all.
Compared to the pain of worrying about things, it was practically a breeze.

I let out a soft sigh, attempting to get my brain out of the doldrums, and leaned back on the bench I was sitting on.

The boiling heat of the day was starting to let up, and at this hour of the late afternoon, the park was starting to empty out.

The blue sky above me showed no indication of transforming into dusk, but the sun was masked by a thin sheet of cloud cover, its fiery anger several measures lower than previously.

The children who occupied the slide and ran around the sandbox a few times earlier were nowhere to be seen.

Now, except for a girl feverishly twirling around on one of the horizontal bars, things were easing back across the landscape.

Like I would've expected.

I took a glance at the park's solar-powered clock. It was beating out the first few seconds of the five o'clock hour, and the echoing of the sirens that accompanied this moment in time had just about faded into obscurity.

It was a signal for children to return home, one invented by God knows who for God knows what reason, but the ones in the park faithfully followed the order.

Grown-ups have a knack for picking up on children who break the rules. Thinking along those lines, I marveled at how the children, holding hands as they crossed the street, showed remarkable intelligence in their decision.

The world we live in is built up out of millions of those little rules. Rules that were all created by the grown-ups.

Attempting to rebel against that was akin to suicide.

Even if children like us, unable to take care of ourselves, began to cry and resist the grown-ups, it would change absolutely nothing in this world.

And for someone like me, enjoying my own world, just letting the day float by with barely a passing thought, nothing seemed ready to change at all.

...Or maybe not.

There was one thing. The pain that seared into my left cheek yesterday had moved to my right cheek today.

It seemed inconsequential enough, but maybe it was worthy of being called "change." It was still stupid, either way.

Even I thought I was being needlessly cranky about this. Maybe I thought it was some kind of earth-shattering discovery. But I was friendless, usually at home alone drowning myself in all kinds of low-class media.

I had a level of knowledge one step above the children of my generation. With that in mind, it was nothing that unusual.

Either way, I joined the children today, as I always did, letting my immature thoughts convince me to protect the "rules" laid out by my mother.

My mingling with the children in this park all day was one of those rules.

In the morning, my mother would come home from work, put me in the bath, cook me some food, then take me to this park, like always.

I would while away the day here until evening, when it was time for my mother to head to work. If she needed me to buy anything, I'd do it. Then I'd clean my room and go to bed.

Living up to that hodgepodge of rules was both my duty and my everything.

Thinking over them, they were all ridiculously simple rules to keep. But I never quite seemed to get the hang of them all, and that'd always anger my mother.

She was angry at me yesterday over forgetting to buy the toilet paper, for example. Today, I broke a cup, which made her fly into another rage.

Whenever she was angry, she would always start punching at me. I'm sure it made her hands hurt as much as it did my cheeks.

The worst of it always came afterward, when I'd have to look at my mother's face as she apologized to me, crying.

But the more I tried to get everything right during the day, the more I wound up swinging and missing.

Even when I tried to make my mother happy, the results were always the exact opposite of what I intended. It was uncanny.

Come to think of it, a bit ago, when the TV remote in the living room broke, my mother fumed and tossed it into the trash, calling it a "defective piece of crap."

That was when I learned what "defective" meant. Someone who couldn't stick to the rules. Something that was no use to anyone.

The scene made the "defective" remote feel remarkably similar to…myself.

The only thing I could do for my mother—so tired from work already—was make her (a) erupt, and (b) cry. There was nothing nondefective about me.

So why didn't my mother ever throw me away?

Shouldn't she be able to throw away a failure like me, just like the defective remote, and replace me with something new?

I don't get it.

Why was I incapable of anything but causing my mother grief every day?

If all I cause her is grief, why was "I" even born?

Why, in the first place, did my mother even bother to…?

Thinking over it, I was caught unawares by something deep in the pit of my stomach contracting painfully.

The physical pain didn't make the tears flow any longer, but now, despite all my requests not to, that feeling made them start to pool deep from behind my lashes.

Oh, crap. I can't cry here. Better think about something else.

If I let someone see me, she might say something again.

I'd be a pain to my mother again. We might not be able to be with each other any longer. What if that happened…?

That would be terrible. I'd never be able to stand it. I couldn't even imagine a world without my mother.

One more hour.

I just needed to sit here, quietly, for another hour until my mother woke up and headed out for work.

Then I'd buy a cup to replace the one I broke, go back home, and just play it cool.

As long as I follow those "rules," I can get through today without saddening my mother any further.

Then I'm sure tomorrow will…

…Will turn out how, *exactly?*

The question, along with a small "Gehh" that was ejected from afar at the same time, brought me back to reality.

My eyes darted around, only to find the girl spinning away at the iron bar was now sprawled out on the ground.

I stared at her. She showed no sign of trying to get up, her arms spread wide as she stared at the heavens.

What happened to her? How'd she wind up like that?

Even a total failure like myself didn't need much time to figure that out.

"Hey! You!"

There was no reply to my command as it echoed slightly across the park.

The eerie silence that followed sent a shiver down my spine that was difficult to describe.

"Oh, is she…?!"

Unable to stand it any longer, I stood, leaping off my post on the bench.

Faced with this all-too-sudden emergency, my head—something no one should ever have to rely upon—was, as I expected, blowing a gasket.

Every inch of it was plastered with the worst-case scenarios I heard or saw on TV or the radio, a torrent of images running across my head.

What if this thing I was seeing before me was the same as what they did on TV recently? That tragic murder scene? The one they had to use a big blue tarp to cover up?

So much seemed to weigh me down at this moment, this second.

The iron bar the girl was gazing at wasn't that high in the air. The problem was how she fell.

I heard there were people who became wheelchair-bound simply because they fell off a chair funny.

Even with playground equipment, if you fell off of it the wrong way, just about anything could happen to you.

"Oh, why is this happening to me…?"

I took another look around. As far as I could see, there wasn't a single grown-up around.

This huge duty of mine, thrust upon me with no advance warning, made me feel like my heart was going to explode.

But I had no time to fret over things, no leeway to sit and worry.

I took another stride, leaping over the sandbox the kids from earlier left in a fairly trashed state. The girl, still on the ground, was now right before my eyes.

Please don't be anything serious, at least.

The hope crossed my mind as I took another all-too-challenging leap.

And just as I did, the girl, completely immobile up to now, whirled herself upward.

Her deep black eyes, a fair match for her medium-length black hair, were dewy as she absentmindedly sized me up.

Ah, thank heavens. It wasn't fatal, then. There was no blood to see, and there was still a healthy pink to her face.

She had a very refined face, actually. No doubt it'd bring her a well-qualified man and a fulfilling family life in the future.

I was just so happy that nothing was serious about—

With an ominous *crack!* a spark of electricity shot into my right ankle.

Given that I was still a mere wisp of an existence, capable of counting my age on two hands, I wouldn't really know what being electrocuted felt like. But it seemed a fair way to describe the pain that stabbed into the very apex of my head.

Oh. Right.

Just a few seconds earlier, I was bounding across the park.

Concerned for the girl's condition and potential future woes, I must have planted down my foot at the wrong angle.

My upper body, moving at high speed, used the outstretched foot as a fulcrum, thrusting it toward the ground below.

It wasn't hard to predict what would happen at the next instant.

I'm sorry, little girl. Try not to stare too much.

"Daaaaaggghhhhhh!"

With a well-chosen, almost theatrical scream, I took a convoluted pose that looked just as well rehearsed as I hit the ground.

If this were a comedy sketch, living rooms across the nation would've been reduced to puddles of laughter by now.

Laughter and applause would have been preferable to *this*, anyway.

Instead, I was in the middle of a completely soundless public park, huddled down low and lacking the comedic timing of knowing when to get back up.

My foot, and the rest of my body, faced searing pain. But, needless to say, that didn't matter to me.

The problem was the base, vulgar feeling known as "shame" that accompanied the pain, hurdling over it like a pole-vaulter.

Think about it. This guy, leaping right in front of you, then letting out an otherworldly wail as he slid to the ground.

…I was out of the game. It was terrifying.

Why did I have to do anything so unplanned, so pointless?

What should I do? Did I need to get up, pat myself down, and run off?

No, I shouldn't. That crack I heard indicated that high-speed travel wasn't going to happen anytime soon.

I would be loping along, all but dragging my bad foot behind me. That much was clear. How could I infuse that innocent girl's mind with yet more dark memories?

Which suggested that the only option was to stay here and wait for time to pass. Was that it?

If I didn't plead my case to her, I would exist in the girl's mind forevermore as "that weird freak who almost pratfalled right into me." I didn't like that much, but today, I had to resign myself to it.

I was fine with that. Really. So come on, time. *Pass by a little quicker for me.*

"Are you hurt?"

How could I possibly be okay?

My entire body hurt. I was painfully embarrassed. And now she was…

"Huh?!"

I looked up, only to find the girl holding a handkerchief right in front of my eyes.

Both of her saucerlike eyes were free of tears. Judging by her expression, she didn't seem interested in trying to report me to the authorities.

"N-no! No, I'm, I'm totally okay! I just kinda tripped a little, is all…Uh. Ha-ha-ha…"

I sat up, mustering the best chuckle I could fake on the spot.

My act didn't make her flee screaming. That was kind of her. But I was still fresh from playing out a live-action blooper reel in front of her.

Just because she held a hand out for me didn't mean my shame was weak enough to let me accept the offering.

Watching me attempt to put myself together in a panic, the girl asked the blisteringly obvious question that stood between us:

"But, but that looked like more than just a trip to me… Looked really painful, too."

The girl's guileless query was like throwing kerosene on the dumpster fire of my shame.

Yes. You're absolutely right. That last fall would probably make it to the top three most gnarly wipeouts of my life.

"I—I'm fine! Really! I trip like this pretty much every day, so I'm kinda used to it, actually."

Nobody like that existed. If they did, they'd be dead in three days.

The reply, laced with equal parts gallantry and massive whoppers of lies, made the girl's face grow even more incredulous.

"Used to it? Um, are you hiding something, maybe…?"

Her eyes peered intently at me, the suspicion now clear across her brows.

"Uh…heh-heh-heh…"

Great. Continuing on like this was just digging my own grave.

She's leaping on me like a coyote, though, isn't she?

Wasn't she motionless on the ground a moment or two ago? Now she's the perfect picture of health.

With that act of hers, you couldn't have paid me enough to tell her, "I tripped because I thought you needed my help." Not at all.

I have a bad feeling about this.

This was already bad, of course, but if I get involved any further with this girl, this would wind up even more of a pain.

If she started spreading rumors about this "weird kid who hurt himself cartwheeling toward me in the park," it would be all hands on deck for me.

At this time in the late afternoon, too, I needed to extract myself out of here, stat. Even if it meant being the weird kid around the neighborhood.

That might leave me with some mental scarring, but so be it. I had to extract myself from this mess. I sighed.

"…All right. I'll tell you the truth."

This seemed to confuse her even further.

"Th-the truth?"

"Yeah. So basically…"

The lingering sense of embarrassment was bringing me close to the breaking point. I bottled it up with an audacious smirk as I continued.

"That thing earlier…That was just me practicing one of my secret moves. Something I can use to…uh, take down bad guys in a single hit."

*   *   *

Silence.

Really, *really* painful silence.

All sound disappeared from the park, as if it were frozen in time. I could see my life gauge plummet as I accepted my new title as the biggest freak in the world.

Right. Now go away. Get freaked out and go away before my face turns into the remains of a forest fire.

That, and just forget about everything that you saw here today. Go home, eat dinner, go to sleep, fall in love, and live out a happy life for me.

But despite my prediction that she would waste no time running for the hills, the girl gave me a wholly unexpected reaction.

"Oh! That really *was* it!"

Her face exuded a blindingly bright curiosity. Sparkles flung out of every pore.

"…Huh?"

"That, that, that's exactly what I *thought* you were doing! W-wow! Now it all makes sense…! Guess you wanna keep your secret moves on the down low, huh? Don't wanna go blabbing about them to everyone, right?!"

The girl was, if anything, five times closer to my face now.

"Y-yeah! Sure!" I blubbered, my head meandering between nodding yes and shaking no.

What kind of hidden fetishes did this girl have, anyway?

I was planning to go down on three strikes just then, only to find myself hitting an inside-the-park home run.

Completely ignoring my fidgety body language, the girl lifted herself up, eyed her surroundings for a moment, and said something even stranger.

"And just between you and me…so was I."

"Um, sorry, what're you talking about?"

I tried to regain some level of distance from her as I asked. The girl took another good look around the park, her voice dropping lower.

"My secret move! I was practicing my secret move!"

She looked deadly serious, even if her words were, by any impartial judgment, less so.

"Huh? Practicing? …You mean that spinning around the bar?"

That was the only thing I could think of.

"Yeah!" Another clean hit, it seemed. "Ooh, I should've guessed you'd know about it!" She was growing more and more excited, her face enrapt in wonder.

I didn't realize there was anything to "know." Why did she think they put bars like that in playgrounds?

And what did that have to do with whatever "secret move" she had in her mind?

Wait. Hang on. Could this girl be…?

"So, um, do you think twirling around on that bar is a secret move…?"

"Yeah! My dad told me. He said, 'Most foes, if you swing on that bar enough, they'll catch on fire and die!' "

There was no doubt in the girl's eyes as she delved further into her fantasy realm.

"I keep messing up just before I go the whole way around. But I got it totally mapped out in my mind. I know I'm gonna do it next time!"

"Uh…cool…"

So there you have it.

Back when she was on the ground, when I thought she broke a leg or something, she was just *picturing* herself doing a full revolution next time. Perfect.

"…Um, so I gotta get home…"

The smirk was a distant memory from my face by now, no doubt, painted over with a dull, pallid expression.

And who could blame me?

There was no telling how much energy I had consumed in the scant few minutes since I noticed this girl.

Probably several months' worth, at least, I imagined.

"What? Already?! But there was so much I wanted to talk to you about..."

Give me a break.

I hated to break it to the girl, but I didn't have enough life force left in my body for a rollicking conversation about deadly attacks using playground equipment.

The pain and fatigue that racked my frame, along with the sheer sense of emptiness this conversation was instilling in me, seemed ready to take physical form behind my back, becoming a giant city-destroying monster of some sort.

"Yeah, uh, it's just about time, so..."

An innocent enough excuse. I gave it with a smile.

"Oooh...," cooed the girl wistfully. I doubted she would continue to try stopping me now.

I looked at the clock. It was just at half past five.

A bit early to go back home, but I had a mission today—a cup to buy, to put it another way.

Considering how much time I wasted here, heading out right now would work out the best timing-wise, anyway.

Standing up with the foot I didn't twist, I gingerly began to place weight on my other leg.

It was painful, as I expected, but not bad enough that I couldn't walk.

If it was hopeless—if it hurt too much to stand—I couldn't even imagine what the girl would say to me then.

"Okay, uh, I'm off."

I tried my best to leave the park behind me at once. "Oooh…!" she replied, the dissatisfaction clear in her groan.

Looking closely, the two eyes that had me in her sights began to display a moistness that wasn't there before.

Oh, crap. I definitely need to head out before this gets even worse.

Fighting off a slight sense of guilt over it all, I gave her a light "Heh-heh!" and began to drag my leg off to the park exit.

"Hey!"

The girl's voice rang out after several steps.

What? What else could she possibly want with me?

I turned around, to find the girl's pained expression now replaced with a soft smile.

"Wanna talk again tomorrow?"

Something about her face, about her words, rendered me speechless.

I wondered if I ever made anyone any promises about tomorrow before at any point in my life.

Nothing I could instantly recall, anyway.

What was I talking about? "Nothing I could instantly recall"? I'm still a kid.

I haven't lived long enough to start burying my memories in oblivion.

"Sure. Tomorrow, right here."

I turned around again and left the park.

Why did I make it so perfunctory? I wasn't sure myself.

My ankle hurt with every step I took along the concrete path. But the way that pain so eloquently spoke of the day's events seemed charming, somehow, at this point.

Better not hurt anything else tomorrow, I thought, attempting to gloss over my true feelings as I casually strolled off.

✳

The neighborhood had begun to show the signs of a quickly advancing evening.

I shuffled the shopping bag from hand to hand to keep my arms from falling asleep, gingerly keeping my weight to one side as I walked. I must be some kind of pro at this by now.

"Good thing I found something nice."

I was still limping as I made my way back home, fresh from a quick trip to the shopping arcade by the station for a new teacup.

The pain certainly made its presence known as I walked, but once I returned home and sat down, it shouldn't be anything unbearable.

A bigger problem was that this ankle made me completely forget about my right cheek.

When the clerk at the shop asked, "Hey, what's up with your face?" I gave the rather uncharacteristic reply of "What, am I that ugly to you?"

That stupid girl.
I have *got* to get back at her somehow tomorrow.

I walked on, silently, stewing in my own juices.

Reaching a road I was well familiar with, turning at an intersection I was well familiar with, crossing an intersection after waiting at the light the same amount of time I always did, I came to the apartment I lived in.

I opened the front door—just as I always did—climbed the

metal stairs, and headed for the farthest door on the second floor.

It wasn't that nice of a building, but once our next-door neighbor moved out two months ago, we'd had the entire floor to ourselves, mostly.

My mother liked that—"Now I don't have to worry about how I look all the time," as she put it—but for someone like me, left alone for much of the night, it honestly left me a tad uneasy. Things like ghosts and ancient curses...I couldn't stand them.

My mother loved that kind of stuff, watching ghost hunter–type shows whose titles alone would make my skin crawl. I really wish she'd stop.

That one the other day, especially, when they were investigating that abandoned hospital...Dahh, I shouldn't try to think about it. Think about something fun. Something fun...

"...Nothing fun around here, really."

Passing by three empty apartments, I finally reached my own home.

I couldn't tell exactly what time it was, but judging by how high the sun was, it probably wasn't too far removed from my usual time.

...But that was really the only thing usual about tonight.

"Huh. The door's open."

In fact, as I approached, it was already halfway ajar. *That's dangerous.*

Thanks to old age, the door needed to be shut tight, or else it'd creak open a little like that. But my mother was aware of that. She had to be.

"Was she in a hurry?"

I didn't pay it much mind as I put a hand on the doorknob.

Until I opened the door and looked up, my mind was running along familiar lines: *Better be more careful when I go out tomorrow.* That kind of thing. I was such a hopeless idiot.

When I turned my face upward, there were two grown-ups in a room illuminated by orange-tinted light.

One I knew well—my mother, still wearing her prim work uniform.

The other I had never seen before, a large man wearing dingy-looking clothing and a ski mask.

"Ah..."

Why hadn't my mother left for work?

My mother *never* wanted to let anyone in our apartment. There was no way she'd invite a guy like this inside.

So why was my mother on her side, teary-eyed, with her hands tied behind her back and a dirty washcloth in her mouth?

Why did this man have some of my mother's favorite jewelry in his grubby hands?

The answer came pretty quickly to me.

But by the time it arrived, it was so late that none of it even mattered any longer.

Without a sound, the man's right hand grabbed my shirt collar and tossed me inside the room.

"Gah!"

Unable to brace myself, my back hit hard against the floor, the air knocked out of my lungs.

At that moment, multiple lights twinkled in front of my eyes, as if an entire corps of press photographers was taking my picture.

I couldn't take a breath.

I had never felt so helplessly unable to breathe in my life.

My mind fell into a panic as I tried to get up. I tried to prop myself with my right hand, only to find it quivering and useless.

My mother, lying down, let out a moan as she attempted to scream.

What? What is she trying to scream at?

What could it be…?

My hazy mind forced my eyes into motion, focusing on the jewelry in the man's left hand as he was about to leave the room.

Yes. That had to be it.

The jewelry my mom slaved on the job every day to finally, victoriously obtain.

And the man was trying to take it somewhere else.

Makes sense, Mom. Who wouldn't scream if someone did that to you?

For a single moment, my right arm found its strength again.

It pushed against the floor, springing my body upward.

On my feet, I used my momentum to lunge at the man's back.

"G-give it back…That…that's not yours…"

But right when it counted the most, I found myself pathetically powerless.

With a clicking of his tongue, the man flung my arm away with the same strength he showed earlier, kicking me back into the room.

"Ngh…!"

Thrown off balance, I found myself facedown on the floor.

My vision grew hazy as I tried to gasp for breath. There was no standing up for me any longer.

I quivered there for a while, silently. Then I heard some metallic clattering from the kitchen.

I couldn't see it, but based on my mother's echoing scream, I understood well enough what that meant.

The knife set. She bought a pretty fancy knife set a while ago. She practically never cooked, either. It stood proudly on the kitchen counter, completely unused. He was probably after something or other in there.

No doubt intending to skewer me before I could take another swipe at him.

One stab would be enough to silence me forever, eliminating the need to keep pushing me off his back. It'd be easy.

And now, with my ear against the floor as I lay there, I had crystal-clear insight on the fact that the man's footsteps were approaching me.

This meant, probably, that I'd be dead in a few minutes. This didn't seem to conjure any particular emotion within me.

At the same time, I can't just lie *here.*

Summoning all the strength that remained, I managed to stand back up. The effort left me panting.

Despite all the suffering I had gone through today, all the pain signals my body transmitted into my brain before were gone.

As I figured, the man standing tall in front of me had a sparkling new knife in his hand.

Swinging blindly with my fists would be nowhere near enough to dispatch him now.

In fact, as far as I could imagine, there wasn't any way I could so much as scratch him.

But I didn't need to worry about that. Just stopping him for a few moments would work well enough.

I glanced at my mother. Tears rained from her eyes as she screamed at me.

Sorry, Mom. I don't think you'll be seeing that jewelry again.
Sorry I was such a failure. An idiot.
But I'm gonna stop this guy for you. Long enough that you can get away, at least.
At the very least, right at the end, I want you to think to yourself: I'm glad I gave birth to him.

I turned back toward the man, releasing the force in both legs in order to ram my entire body into the enormous frame of the man facing me—
I tried to, anyway.

The moment I took a step forward, the man was slammed against the wall.
My mother had rammed herself against him first—the no-longer-new knife buried deeply in her chest.
That took me a little longer to comprehend.
My mother tried to plead something with her eyes, her face twisted in pain, but all I could do was stare dumbly at her.
It was only when the man removed the knife from her, fresh blood flying in the air, that something snapped in my mind.

I couldn't hear anything any longer, but I think I probably shouted something.
But it couldn't have been that long of an interval between me leaping at him and him stabbing me in the stomach and stomping me to the ground.

I lay there, lined up nearly alongside my mother, attacked by the strange sensation of drowning in a frigid pool of blood.
My mom, through the tears, seemed like she was trying to tell me something through the gag. But, in the end, it never came across.

I was in an unknown town.

As far as I could see, there was nothing I could recognize in it.

There were no familiar colors in the sky above me. The only thing I could see in the inky blackness was a single unnervingly large sphere of some sort.

Yes. This was night.

I…or, really, any children like me…didn't know about the night.

A world for grown-ups, partitioned away from the day, brimming with light.

A world just for adults, one I must never set foot upon.

A world of darkness, one that swallowed up my mother and took her away at regular intervals.

…I always hated the night.

The sound of my shoe against the concrete rebounded off the walls of the buildings, echoing tinnily against my ears with each step forward.

The wind that blew was cold and uninviting, whispering something dark and ominous to me as it breezed past.

Whenever the miasma of crisp neon in the night entered the corner of my vision, I turned away. It felt like something I must never look at, lest something awful happen.

*   *   *

It felt gross. Nausea began to take me.

I was seized by something resembling dizziness as I kept going down the road, not knowing where it would end.

"Hey, kid, you shouldn't be here."

Suddenly, it felt like someone was whispering in my ear.

"You're still a kid, aren't you? You have no idea what the night is like. Get on back home, okay?"

"...Like you've got a right to say that. What do *you* know?"

"Oh, everything. I'm a grown-up."

The voice, which seemed permanently attached to my ear, began to gradually enrage me.

"Stop treating me like a kid!"

The whispering voice began to emit a shrill, piercing noise.

It sounded a bit like someone laughing, a bit like a snake sticking its tongue out at me.

"You're a hopeless case, aren't you? You just blundered your way blindly into here. I can tell. So listen. What I'm trying to tell you is, you have no comprehension of the most important thing in the world."

*   *   *

The voice was shriller than before. It felt like its lips were practically touching my earlobe.

"The most important thing?"

The moment I asked, the echoing steps stopped. I didn't stop walking, but the sound muted itself out.

I looked around, surprised, only to find the shimmering neon, the building walls, even the moon floating above whirling around me.

"What's happening?!" I shouted. But I could no longer hear my own voice.

A boundless darkness, a black that no light could shine through. Even my own trembling frame seemed to melt into the void around me.

"Can't you see them? The 'lies' that infused themselves into this place?"

I felt like the whispering voice was coming from inside me now.

"Grown-ups make the lies creep into the darkness. That's how they protect their own hearts and minds."

I couldn't understand what it meant. I felt boxed in, unable to breathe. *Get me out of here.*

"Do you understand, boy? This is the night. A grown-up world you have no clue about."

…What are *grown-ups?*
Why did my mother ever have to venture into that world…?

"Do you want to know? If you want to know…you must forget about that pure, unblemished heart of yours."

Forget my heart?

"Yes. In the deep, dark, solitary world of the night, there is no need for a heart at all. All you need are 'lies.'"

My consciousness, which I had so valiantly tried to keep intact, finally began to give on me.
Everything I owned felt like it was being melted into the darkness.
The final words were the only thing that registered in my dwindling consciousness, seeping into my fading heart.

"You must deceive them all, boy."

YOBANASHI DECEIVE 2

Summer was over.

The stifling heat and the cries of a million insects all vanished somewhere without a trace, leaving me alone.

I lay flat in my room—really more of a storage closet—continuing to live and breathe, nothing to do today or any other day.

After my mother was gone, I was passed around from this place to that for a while before winding up here.

The couple who owned this building I was in were related to my mother, apparently. Not by blood. Really, it couldn't have been a shallower relationship.

Two months have passed.

I, the lone survivor, didn't even think about dying.

The experience made me realize that any reason I had for living, or dying, was defined purely on the basis of me having a mother.

Even if I died here, what would that accomplish?

No matter what I did, I would never see my mother again. It was all meaningless.

The only thing that didn't change was that I was still my mother's son.

If I, left alone, did anything to cause trouble for other people—especially dying, most of all—I'd never be able to explain it to her.

It was nearly impossible for me to stand.

So I kept living on as the meaningless days passed, one after the other.

That seemed like the most intelligent approach to take.

I was lying on my back, staring listlessly at the ceiling, when a chill breeze from the open window pushed into the room.

If I was sure about anything right now, it was that this couldn't last.

I needed to become stronger, I needed to find work, I needed to eat.

But before all that, I needed to grow up...

The moment the words "grow up" flashed across my mind, I felt like something was squirming around within my heart.

I sat up with a shiver. It seemed to pass. No pain, no difficulty breathing.

"What was that...?"

Maybe I shouldn't have left the window open.

If I was catching the flu or something, that was seriously bad news.

I didn't have the impression that the landlords here were particularly fond of me.

Me breaking into a fever would make them scowl at me even more, no doubt.

If I wanted to be fully prepared, I should probably take some cold medicine or something, shouldn't I? Hmm.

I think I remembered them telling me where the medicine cabinet was when they were giving me their very hurried tour of the place.

I didn't recall the exact location, but if they bothered to show it to me, they must have intended for me to use it.

"Hmm...Maybe I should ask."

Asking for permission along with confirmation would kill two birds with one stone. *Let's nip this in the bud before it gets worse.*

I stood up and left the room.

Even the hallways of this place exuded elegant refinement. It was positively extravagant, especially compared to the dingy place I used to live.

Although, really, it wasn't like I could expect any kind of regular family here, either.

Maybe this label of "extravagant" is based on the biases created by my upbringing. If someone told me this place was normal, I wouldn't have anything to fire back with.

Still, though.

I never said it out loud, and I never intended to, but the bits of décor installed here and there, the works of art hung on the front-door hallway—I wouldn't exactly call much of it in good taste.

Walking down the hall, I went face-to-face with an ominous-looking bit of sculpture. I couldn't tell whether it was supposed to represent an animal or something, but there it was.

Probably some kind of souvenir from one overseas trip or another.

I knew the sculptor wasn't at fault for it or anything, but as the person who had to dust it every day, I wished I could have called him up and said, "Couldn't you have made this a little less intricate?"

Passing it by, I opened the door to the kitchen and went inside.

It was almost time for dinner. If the lady who ran the house—I called her my aunt, because I couldn't call her "ma'am" forever—was there, that would've made things simple for me.

But my aim must have been off. Nobody was around in the kitchen, and judging by the pile of dishes taken out of the dishwasher, dinner wasn't going to be ready anytime soon.

"No one, huh...? Hmm. Now what...?"

I didn't quite have the nerve to run up to my aunt's room and ask her where the medicine was. But it made me feel awkward to just sit and wait for her, too.

Luckily, though, my trip to the kitchen helped jog my memory of the location a little.

I thought I remembered it being in one of the drawers in the tea cabinet.

No point obsessing over it all day. I'll just try opening a few and see what pops out. If I find it, I'll take a dose and go back to my room.

I took a step toward the large wooden tea cabinet that loomed large on the other side of the kitchen.

But—and there's no reason why I shouldn't have just ignored it—for some reason, I shot a quick glance toward the pile of dishes.

Next to the stack of elegantly designed kitchenware, there was a single knife laid on top of a washcloth.

It was the same type that man used to stab my mother back on that day.

A shiver ran down my spine as my heart skipped a little.

It wasn't *the* knife that took my mother's life, of course. This one was well-worn and clearly used, for example.

I reached out to have a closer look.

Grabbing the handle and picking it up, I realized the knife had some heft to it.

It was every bit the equal of the rest of the house's furnishings. It must have cost someone a bundle.

"…Geez, Mom. You bought something as nice as this, and you died without ever using it…"

My mother was remarkably chatty the day she bought that cutlery set.

She pretty much forgot about it the next day, but at the time, her eyes practically sparkled as she went on about it, like, "I can make some really nice dishes with these" and so on.

Thinking about that subjected me to a sudden onrush of loneliness.

My mother's face, her voice, her scent floated into my mind, as fresh as new.

Mom...

"Yaaaaggghhh!!"

The scream threw me out of my trance.

Turning my head, I saw my aunt at the edge of the kitchen, just about ready to start with dinner.

Her face was taut, like a ghost just crossed her path. Abject fear was written across it.

Oh, no.

The sight of me holding a knife must've startled her.

"Oh, I, I'm sorry! I was just looking at it a little!"

Hurriedly, I placed the knife back on the washcloth and held my palms out at my aunt, virtually in self-defense.

I had no intention of attacking her at all, of course, so this seemed like the best plan of action.

Hopefully, this would calm her down a bit. I didn't want to give the wrong impression and have her call the police on me. That would be bad.

But.

Not only did my aunt not breathe a sigh of relief—her face grew even paler, more pallid, as she began to tremble.

Something was clearly wrong with her. I had no idea what was paralyzing her with fear so badly.

Just as I opened my mouth, searching for some way to defuse the situation, my aunt began speaking in a half scream, half gibber.

"Wh-why, why are you…?! Do, do you have some kind of grudge against us?!"

A grudge…? I had no recollection of anything like that.

If anything, I was honestly glad they gave me free room and board.

"No, I…Um, if you could just calm down a sec…"

I still couldn't fathom my aunt's behavior, but in a valiant attempt to ease this misunderstanding, I took a step or two toward her.

I was still waving my open palms left and right at her. I couldn't have possibly looked hostile to anyone…

"Ahh—aggghghhh!! G-get away from me!"

The effort was in vain. With a crazed shriek, my aunt made a flying dash for the hallway.

"Ahh! H-hey, wait a minute!"

I wasn't sure my aunt heard me as she opened the front door and ran off to points unknown.

The only thing that echoed across the elegant manor was the loud slamming of the door behind her.

Ah, crap. Crap, crap, crap.

This was getting way out of hand.

I had no intention at all of doing…whatever I did. This had to be some kind of gigantic mistake.

"Wh-what should I do?! Ahhh…"

I stood there for a minute, shaking my head at myself, hand to my temple. This inexplicably failed to reverse the course of time.

Great. Why did I have to go and do something like that *again?*

I should have just stayed there, in my room, and been a good kid.

If I didn't think about something as stupid as taking some

medicine as insurance against the flu, none of this would have ever happened...

I shot a cold stare at the knife, ruing its very existence.

It was *that* thing's fault, too.

How much grief is it going to put me through until it's happy? Something about the elegant blade, glinting in glee at my misery, made me want to scream with anger.

I knew it wouldn't accomplish anything, but I swiftly took up the handle again.

Let's just throw this away somewhere. No—it'd be better for me if I sold it off. My mind ran circles around itself for a moment before I caught sight of the blade's mirrorlike surface.

"...Huh?!"

I was astonished. The impossible sight before me made me drop the knife at once, sending it clattering to the floor.

I brought a hand up to feel my face. Nothing seemed wrong with it. There was no way to confirm what I just saw unless I took another look.

Out of the kitchen I fled, passing by that tacky sculpture again as I tore into the bathroom.

The moment I made it in, I found myself in shock once more at the sight in the mirror above the sink.

"Wh-why?"

The sight before me wasn't the familiar one I knew. It was my mother, in the flesh.

If this were me being reunited with my real mother, I would've immediately flown into her arms.

But that could never happen. My mother was dead.

It was strange, though, how coolheaded my mind was when faced with this bizarre sight.

I approached the mirror, giving myself a pinch on the cheek.

The face itself was beyond a doubt my mother's, but the feedback my fingertips gave me indicated something else.

I spent a few more moments staring at the mirror.

Opening and closing my mouth a few times, I saw my mother make the exact same motion in the mirror.

There was no denying it. It was me.

What could have caused this? I had no clue whatsoever. But here I was. In the form of my mother.

The moment the thought struck me, I heard the gears begin to click together in my mind.

Is *this* what my aunt saw before she screamed her head off and bolted?

Well, no wonder *she was acting like that.*

Just when she went down to the kitchen for dinner, she saw her dead relative standing there, well-polished knife in "her" hand.

I couldn't blame her for running. If that were me, I would've hugged her, but…

But what was I going to do now?

Staring at the mirror and whispering "I've been dying to see you" was both nonproductive and more than a little creepy.

I needed to regain my original looks as soon as I could.

My aunt was probably summoning the authorities right now. I didn't have the time to stand around here, looking like (also, at) my mom.

Then again, would the police really come running if a hysterical woman went up to them and said, "My dead half-sister-in-law (or whatever it was) is in the kitchen with a knife!"?

That didn't seem likely. No doubt they'd just brush her off and send her on her way. I still had some time to work with.

Taking yet another close look at my mother in the washbasin mirror, I failed to find any button I could press to go back to normal, nor any other obvious solution out of my dilemma.

When did I even *start* looking like this?

That reflection I glimpsed when I first picked up the knife was myself. No doubt about that.

And I gave my aunt the scare of her life just a moment or two after that. Somehow, I transformed in the stretch of that single instant.

But why, though...?

There was one cause and effect I could think of, actually.

"N-no way..."

I closed both of my eyes and attempted to follow the thread.

The one thing I did in that instant.

The way that I "recalled" my mother's looks, her voice, her scent.

Maybe "recalling" another "target" would bring me back to normal.

But.

If *that* was all it took for an idiot like me to shapeshift at will, we'd have an entire planet full of shapeshifters. IDing people would be impossible.

I didn't have much hope, to be honest.

But let's focus here. Concentrate.

Think about a look, a sound, a scent...and "recall" it.

...Around thirty seconds passed, I supposed.

"Okay."

I didn't know whether it'd be enough time or not, but I opened my eyes.

"...Whoa! Serious?!"

The image of my mother in the mirror was gone without a trace.

In its place was someone else. The girl I encountered in that park around two months ago.

Her shape, her skin color, her striking eyes…Everything I remembered about the girl was there, unchanged, in its full glory.

"Wow! What the hell…? This is amazing!"

I don't think I had experienced this kind of "fun" in my entire life before this point.

In fact, I *knew* I hadn't.

That was how shocking, how bizarre, and how curiosity-stoking this phenomenon thrust before me seemed.

I knew it was a waste of time, but I couldn't stave off the urge to find out what I could turn into next. It was like all the youthful mischief I bottled up during my life was being uncorked in a single afternoon.

The eyes of the girl in the mirror began to sparkle, just as she did when she talked about her "secret move."

This must be it. How you felt at that moment.

No wonder you were so eager to latch on to me like that.

Come to think of it, I never saw her after that day—after I made that promise.

If I ever get to meet her again, I'm gonna give her the surprise of the millennium.

I skipped around the bathroom a little, enjoying life as a girl for a few more moments, until I heard someone unlatching the front door.

My body froze on the spot. An uncomfortable sweat began to pour from my brow.

Straining my ears, I could hear my aunt shouting, "In here! There's a strange woman…!"

Wow. Smart move on her part.

I wasn't a "ghost"; I was an "intruder." That was the trick she needed to get the cops in here.

Playtime was clearly over for now.

This really wasn't any time for playing in the first place, admittedly, but now it was even *less* that time.

Luckily, it sounded like they were playing it safe. I didn't hear any heavy footsteps tromping their way down the hallway yet. Better get back to the original me before then. Having her intruder vanish might put my aunt in an awkward position with the police, but there wasn't much I could do about that.

I'll just have to atone for it later, somehow.

I closed my eyes. The darkness spread before them.

I focused as much as I could, straining to recall my shape, my scent, my voice…

Here I am…!

"…Um. Uh-oh."

The sweat began to form waterfalls.

Crap. I couldn't recall *myself* at all.

How little interest did I *have* in myself all my life, anyway?

Thinking about it, I realized I never had my picture taken. I had a habit of avoiding myself in the mirror, too.

And now that we were on this topic, I never thought much about my own voice, and that went *double* for how I smelled.

I held out against hope as I opened my eyes. I wasn't disappointed. Just as I expected, the same pale girl as before greeted me.

Her face stiffened further as she heard the creak of multiple feet against the wooden floor.

I'd *love* for the cops to catch me looking like this. And what a huge pain it'd be on the *real* girl, too.

I scrambled to think of someone else to turn into, but with my mind about to short circuit, there was no way to focus on anything any longer.

*   *   *

"I—I gotta hide...!"

There was a separate room on the other side of the chamber that housed the actual bathtub and shower.

It wouldn't suffice as a hiding spot for more than a few moments, really, but it beat standing right in front of the sink like this.

My mind made up, I sprang into action.

Then, on my first step, I tripped on the edge of the bathmat and fell to the floor.

"Ow!!"

A dull, yet intense pain erupted from my back.

Spotting my yelp, the multiple presences mere feet away from me in the hallway stormed into the bathroom.

As I expected, several police officers filed in, glaring down at what I presumed was still a young girl on the floor. My heart froze.

I had no idea how I was going to apologize to her for this.

Assuming I'd ever have the chance. If people found out I had this power, they'd instantly brand me as the cause behind all this furor.

I couldn't even imagine how much of a pain in the ass *that* was going to be.

This was all my fault. I couldn't even begin to apologize. *I am such a careless idiot.*

Just as I was about to drown in my own self-pity, one of the officers extended a hand out to me, the others still on high alert.

"You all right, kid? What happened in here?"

"Oh, uh, nothing. I just kinda tripped on the mat here..."

I told him the truth...somewhat selectively. Yes, that's definitely what happened in the last half second, officer.

"Oh. Okay. Um...is there anyone else besides you?"

"No...," I said, shivering for a moment.

Then, from behind the cops, my aunt fearfully peeked in at me.

It's over. I'm dead.

I was sure the sight of this mystery girl would give her a heart attack.

After that, all the dominoes would fall at once.

I'd be taken away somewhere, interrogated...and I didn't even want to imagine what came after that.

But despite my dreadful expectations, my aunt's reaction defied all of them.

"Shuuya, what are you *doing*?"

"Huh?"

Being called by my name was usually nothing of particular note. But in these circumstances, it held major meaning.

I clambered back to my feet and stared into the mirror. And there I was. Back to my old self, a little teary-eyed.

"Sh-Shuuya? What's going on with you?"

I didn't respond. I was too busy pondering why I was back to myself.

"...Pain!"

The conclusion seemed a tad ironic to me.

That bolt of pain that shot across my back.

The one reaction I had to that...was nostalgia. Familiarity.

I thought I was used to the pain. But that was a grave mistake.

To me, pain was something I needed to truly feel like myself. The only identity I really had.

The idea of pain being my only insight into myself...Is that how little my own mind cared about me?

As everyone else in the room looked on worriedly, I began laughing at myself. At the inanity of it all.

...The power to pose as someone else. To deceive people.

My first encounter with that eerie force was something I couldn't have been more open to accepting.

The air felt heavy within the car.

The heater ensured we were kept at a comfortable temperature, but there was no lively conversation, no particular sense of comfort.

The rhythmical beat of light and dark from the passing streetlights brought the car the only sense of life it had.

I sighed, lightly, so that my aunt wouldn't notice.

I was never that good in cars, anyway. I was bad. *Really* bad. Really, any kind of rideable object. Seesaws and stuff were fine, but when it got up to cars and trains, I faced serious digestive trouble.

My lack of experience riding in them might have something to do with it. But there must've been something wrong with my inner-ear canals or something. My sense of balance was incredibly weak, and that made me sick to my stomach.

I remember how my mother got the insane idea to put me on a roller coaster once. That was one thing I could never quite forgive her for. It was awful. So fast, so shaky, all spinny and dazzly…It made no sense to me why anyone would enjoy that.

By the time I felt the contents of my stomach make a dash for my esophagus, I was prepared to kill myself right there. If I was going to debase myself in public, might as well go all the way, I thought.

I managed to avoid the worst-case scenario, luckily. But I had zero desire to repeat that experience again.

Regardless, we left home about forty minutes ago.

The car was headed for a special-care facility that would be my next home.

Why did this happen? There were several reasons I could

think of. But that particular incident—the day I discovered my powers—probably sealed my fate.

Ever since that first day I fully awoke to my abilities, my aunt began to make clear and obvious efforts to avoid me whenever possible.

I never discussed my freaky new abilities with her, of course, and nobody ever found out about them in the end.

Or so I surmised, at least. But my aunt must have assumed the worst-case scenario. The next day, our elegant manor was visited by a string of self-styled exorcists, or spirit dispellers, or something like that.

These guys were all clearly frauds to any impartial observer, but my aunt seemed to like all of them, swallowing up everything they said about orbs and auras and electrostatic levels and so on.

That was the beginning of the end for me. It turned out I, as it went, was the cause of all this terror and eeriness. You can guess the rest.

I was planning to leave the whole time, of course, if I was getting in the way. It's not like I was going to miss the place much, either.

If there was anything I did regret, it was the way I never made up for any of it. And how could I? How could a kid like me make up for triggering as much chaos as I did back there?

I wanted to, somehow, if I could. But right now, I couldn't think of a single way.

Just as I let out another sigh, the car lumbered to a halt.

"We're here," my aunt said, exiting the car as I checked out the surroundings. "Time to get out."

The light-brown building on the other side of the windshield must have been the "facility" my aunt was talking about.

The way she put it, it was a home for kids like me with no close relatives to turn to.

"I figured," my aunt said with an awkward smile as she tried to sell me on it, "it'd be best if you were together with more kids your age."

There was nothing more annoying in my life than other kids my age.

To someone like me, who had yet to make a single friend his entire life, the house before my eyes seemed like little more than a zoo.

After locking the car, my aunt looked at her watch.

"Wait here a moment, okay? I need to talk to the staff inside."

"Huh? Um, okay."

My aunt disappeared behind the front door, leaving me alone. My body, warmed by the heat of the car, began to shiver in the northerly winds.

The experience made me feel a little sentimental. Which was crazy. I *never* got that way.

But I didn't have long to enjoy it. The wind began to kick up, howling, chilling my bones with astonishing force.

"Eesh, this is cold! How long's she gonna make me wait out here…?"

Not being particularly stout of frame, the blustering wind made my body shiver.

I wouldn't have minded so much if she was in and out in a couple of minutes. When that grew to ten or twenty or so, though, that was a different story.

C'mon, lady, why'd you have to take me out of the car if you were going in by yourself first? Didn't you think at all? And you even locked the door so I couldn't go back inside. Thanks a lot. I'm going to freeze out here, waiting by the door.

I paced around a little, trying to stave off the cold. The effort was a failure, all the heat in the world actively avoiding my presence. Time passed.

"...Argh, I can't *do* this! It's too cold! I'm gonna die out here!"
I scoped out my surroundings one more time as I complained to myself. I didn't know what I had been expecting. There certainly wasn't a space heater nearby.
This is what I get for slapping on whatever was lying around my room this morning. I *knew* I should've worn another layer or two.
I'm not asking for a fancy padded ski jacket or anything. Just some gloves, at least...

As I contemplated this, I suddenly saw a scarf thrust in front of me.
Sure. That'll do. Any port in a storm.
It was right when I breathed a sigh of relief, smiled serenely, and reached out to pick it up that I realized what was strange about this.
Just an instant before—the blink of an eye—there was nobody else here. Now there was, like nothing could be more typical.
I reared back with an ugly-sounding "Agghh!"
As I did, I noticed the person offering me the scarf was a girl, one around the same age I was.

She had a pair of large purple earmuffs and a heavy, warm-looking coat on. It all looked nice on her, but her hair was a mess, going off in all directions and sticking out into the air in spots.
I almost thought she was a boy at first, but given the skirt she was wearing, it seemed safe to assume otherwise.

My shocked reaction made the girl flinch a bit. Then she sheepishly glared at me.

"I'm *trying* to give this to you, you know."

"Uh..."

My hesitance was starting to annoy her.

"It'd be weird for someone right next to me to die, all right? So I thought I'd give this to you!"

"Agh! Um...oh. Well, thanks! Ha-ha! Guess I might as well..."

I reached for the scarf. "That's what you should've been doing all along," she snorted.

Maybe it was just my imagination. It really *did* seem like she popped up out of nowhere.

I still had my concerns about that, but at a time like this, it'd probably be better to just shut up and take it.

Just like the rest of the short-haired girl's outfit, the scarf was perhaps a little too fancy to be kids' wear.

A quick examination revealed a label that prominently featured a major brand.

My mother had a watch from that same brand.

I remembered how rarely she actually wore it. It was so expensive—or expensive-looking, at least—that it spent most of its life deep in a drawer somewhere.

"I, um, I dunno if I should take this from you..."

I tried to smile politely. The short-haired girl clearly didn't appreciate the gesture.

"I'm *trying* to help you..."

"Oh, no! I really appreciate it! Really! But this is a really nice scarf, isn't it? You shouldn't just be giving it to people like this."

The girl gave me a confused gaze.

"What, this is...expensive, or...?"

"Oh! Didn't you know? Umm...well, look, I'm fine, okay?"

I pushed the scarf back at the girl. She wordlessly accepted it, the frustrated dejection written clearly on her face. Her eyes focused on it for a moment…and then on me, as she began to wrap it around my neck herself.

"Whoa!"

"I'll let you borrow it anyway. You look really cold. I've been watching you for a while."

A lot more obstinate than I thought she'd be.

I wasn't much in the mood for it, but it wasn't like I was going to indignantly strip it off my head in front of her.

From the neck down, I could feel my body warm up a little. Then, in a few short moments, you couldn't have paid me enough money to give the scarf back.

"Aw…Well, thanks. This is really good."

That's what buying brand name gets you. It was shockingly warm.

I didn't have much of a grasp of how much things cost in general, but I reasoned that the scarf must've been worth shelling out for a little.

But I was left in my reverie of cozy warmth for just a few scant moments before the meaning behind the words "watching you for a while" finally registered in my mind.

"Say, uh, where were you watching me from, though?"

"Huh? What do you mean, where? I was right next to you…"

The short-haired girl reached that point in her reply before something dawned on her. Her face grimaced, a soft moan escaping her lips.

"Um…I'm sorry, did I say something I shouldn't have?"

I asked it carefully, worried that I was hitting a sore point of some kind with her. "Not really," she gruffly replied. "People've said that a lot lately. Like, 'since when were *you* there,' kind of thing."

It made sense, as I gauged her gruff, annoyed-looking

demeanor. She didn't act like she particularly enjoyed conversation. Maybe she just didn't stand out much.

"Yeah…I mean, you kind of surprised me because it seemed like you appeared out of thin air, kinda. I thought you were a ghost or something for a sec."

It was a joke. But in hindsight, I wasn't sure that intention came across. I added a strained "ah-ha-ha" at the end, but the girl still reddened before my eyes.

"Ngh…"

Tears began to come out. It was, of course, the first time I ever made a girl cry in my life.

"Ahhhh!! I'm sorry! I'm just kidding! I'm kidding, okay?! I didn't feel that way at *all*, all right?!"

It was a commendable effort on my part, I thought, but it was already too late.

The girl stood there, sniffling to herself, interjecting little attacks on me as she did—"You're not kidding," "I'll get you back for that," "I swear," and so on.

Great. I screwed everything up yet again.

I recalled how my mother warned me about girls. "Watch out," she had said. "They can be pretty delicate creatures." I didn't realize *this* was what she meant.

"Umm…umm…"

This is going to be my home *starting today. What am I doing, here in front of it?*

If someone saw me right now, I might start getting treated like a problem child before I even made it through the door. I whirled my head around, checking for eyewitnesses. Once to the right, once to the left—and then, just as I was about to look right again, something startled me.

The short-haired girl, sobbing in front of me a moment ago, had vanished without a trace.

*   *   *

"Huh?! When did she…?!"

It was even more of a shock to me than when she first appeared.

If I offended her to the point where she couldn't take it anymore and ran off, she still would've been visible in the distance somewhere. And unless she was wearing spongy slippers or something, I should've been hearing some footsteps.

But no matter where I looked, I couldn't find any evidence of her.

It was weird. That short-haired girl just up and disappeared without any warning. It happened too fast to describe it in any other way.

"You're kidding me…"

I rubbed my eyes, unable to believe what just happened.

"*You're* kidding *me!*"

The voice startled me all over again.

In the second or two I was rubbing my eyes, the short-haired girl was right back where she was standing before.

Normally, this experience would've made me scream out loud. The only reason I didn't was because it happened so suddenly, my mind couldn't wrap itself around it.

It was a good thing I didn't. If I raised my voice in front of this girl, still crying her heart out in front of me, I'd probably get slapped for it.

But as I contemplated this, I was greeted by an even more incredible sight, one that made my jaw clamp down in self-defense.

The short-haired girl's body, from her feet to the bottom of her knees just below where her skirt ended, was gradually fading away from existence.

That was enough to make even me gasp a little. I meant it as a joke, but maybe I was right—she could be a ghost after all.

*   *   *

…Wait a minute.

Could she really be something like that?

I had a near-death experience of my own, not too long ago. Maybe she started talking to me because she thought I was one of *her* kind…or something.

"You probably think I'm a ghost, don't you?"

She was going to make *me* break down in tears if she kept that line of questioning up.

I was paralyzed, shivers shooting up and down my spine as I scrambled to keep myself together.

"Ah…Ha! Ha-ha-ha! Oh, come onnnn! I don't think anything like that at all! C'mon, we're all friends here, right?!"

As I expected, I wasn't capable of much coherent speech.

My legs began to tremble. I couldn't blame her if she noticed how petrified I was.

"Friends…?"

She continued to sniffle a bit.

"Y-yeah! I mean…We're both kinda the same, aren't we? Like…uh…"

How were we the same? At least *I* had both of my legs intact. *She* was floating wispily in the air. *I am such an idiot.*

The girl looked less than convinced as she stared at me.

Great. She's gonna kill me. I'll be cursed and buried alive or burned to ashes or something.

If I had known this was going to happen, I would've borrowed a "magic amulet" or two from one of my aunt's fraudulent exorcists.

It wasn't the idea of death that scared me so much as how I had no idea what she'd do to me next.

Just when the panic was about to make me start bawling, my mind conjured up a brilliant idea.

*   *   *

"Oh! I know! Lemme show you this trick I've got! And once you see it, then...you know, we can be friends, then! Okay?"

"Huh?" the girl replied, edging back a little. "What're you talking about?" It wasn't the response I hoped for my teary-eyed pleadings. No turning back now, though. I kept going.

"J-just watch me, all right?! I promise you won't regret it!" The girl's face indicated to me that she had no trust in me whatsoever. I paid it no mind as I closed my eyes and tried to concentrate.

Since that fateful day when I discovered my ability, I tried using it a handful of times, taking care not to have my family discover it.

Thinking about the rough outlines of someone—their voice, their scent, their shape—was enough to let me transform into them.

After a few test runs to satisfy my curiosity, I began to have a general picture of the ground rules. First, I couldn't turn myself into inanimate objects. I tried turning into an airplane once—I figured it'd be fun to go on a little trip—but when I opened my eyes, the only thing I saw in the mirror was a demented boy with his arms outstretched in the air.

I'd never even seen a plane up close in person, much less taken a ride in one. It would have been a much bigger surprise if it actually worked. Plus—really, trying to become an airplane *indoors*? What was I thinking? How was I going to pay for the house I'd inevitably level in the process?

After a bit more experimentation, I came to the realization that I could only transform into living things I've (a) physically met before, and (b) could conjure a clear image of in my mind. Being able to transform didn't mean I could engineer vast changes in terms of body size or musculature, either.

There was only so much I could do by myself, though, and there was a lot I still didn't know. But now that I was in this situation, it was the only thing I could turn to.

Simply "recall" someone I thought this girl would enjoy seeing, and...

Sorry I keep relying on you, girl from the park.

When I opened my eyes, I saw the short-haired girl staring blankly at me, mouth wide open.

Hopefully *that* went over well. I began to sweat a little.

"Wh-what do you think? Neat, huh?"

The girl began quivering.

Whoops. Maybe not so much. It's all over for me. I began reciting my final prayers in my mind when the girl finally spoke.

"Yeah...Pretty neat!"

Her eyes began to sparkle, just as mine did when I first used this ability. I called off the last rites and sighed to myself in relief.

"Y-you think so?! Whew...Great."

"What *is* that, though...?"

"Um...How to put it? I guess you could say I can transform into anybody I want, maybe?"

"Wowww...!"

The astonishment in her voice was palpable.

Sweet. Now we're back in business! That was a lot easier than I expected. If I can keep this up, maybe she'll let me out of this alive.

"Can you show me anyone else?"

"...Um?"

The short-haired girl must've liked it more than I thought. She eagerly awaited my next transformation, eyes focused squarely on me.

"Uh, sure! Yeah! Okay, who should I do next...?"

I didn't have many more tricks up my sleeve, though. In fact, the only other member of my repertoire I was confident I could break out at the drop of a hat was my mother.

Oof. My total lack of social relationships was really coming back to bite me now. I probably should've interacted some more with the kids in the park.

Becoming my mother was not at all something I wanted to do...but so be it.

Sorry, Mom. I just don't want this ghost to kill me, that's all. Just one more time...!

"...All right. Here goes."

"Uh-huh..."

I shut my eyes and let it all enter my recall. Her shape, her voice, her scent...

Unlike the girl from the park, I had no problem remembering my mother at all. That was partly why this was so much more difficult for me. I opened my eyes.

"...What do you think?"

"Ooooh!"

The short-haired girl's reaction was the brightest I had seen from her yet. She accentuated it with a few seconds of enthusiastic clapping. It made me a little self-conscious.

"Ha-ha-ha! Yeah, uh...thanks."

...Well, look at that. She's not so bad after all.

The blunt hostility she greeted me with at first was now firmly in the past, at least. Maybe there were some decent ghosts out there after all. And a ghost like this, I really *could* be friends with, maybe.

"Huh?"

Taking a glance downward, I noticed that the bottoms of the girl's legs had reappeared.

"Um...what? Is there something wrong with my legs?"

The girl gave me a questioning look.

"Uh...no. Not really."

"Not 'really'? You weirdo."

She shrugged, apparently not paying it too much mind. I wanted to argue that we were *both* weirdoes in a way, but I resisted, not wanting to say the wrong thing and trample on her delicate heart again.

Then she brought her hand out to me.

"Okay, then...Yes."

"Yes?"

"No, I mean...Friends! We're friends, okay? So shake on it."

She waved her hand a little bit closer to my midsection.

Ah. Right. I forgot about it in the midst of my wild panicking, but I did mention something about that, didn't I?

"Oh, uh...Sure. Right. Um..."

I should have just taken her hand, but in my infinite intelligence, I hesitated. Instead, the girl grabbed my right hand and forced it into her own. Then she grinned.

"Good. Friends, then."

Something about it intensely embarrassed me. I felt like my head was going to catch on fire. *This is the first friend I've ever made, isn't it? Even I can make one of them.* The kind of friend you can play with together, like the kids in the park I resented so much.

"S-sure!"

I firmed up my grip a little and smiled as broadly as I could. It was a moment to remember—myself and my very first friend, the short-haired "ghost" girl.

"Hey, what's your name, by the way?"

"Oh!"

I exclaimed my surprise out loud. I couldn't go around proclaiming she was my friend if I didn't even know her name. Her eyebrows arched downward.

"Also, how long are you gonna hold my hand?"
I flung my hand back out of embarrassment.

"Oh! Right! Ha-ha-ha! My name. Um, my name's Shuuya. Shuuya Kano."
"Hmm..."
The short-haired girl nodded to herself for a moment.
"Wh-what about you?"

"My name is Kido..."

"Yeaaaaaggghhhhh!!"
Just as the girl was giving her name, I heard a now-familiar scream from the front door.
I turned around in a flash. I knew what I'd see there, and I wasn't disappointed—my aunt stood bolt upright, all but ready to foam at the mouth.
...Oh. Right. I was waiting on her.
"Wh-why're you following me *here*?! You chased me here, didn't you?! *Didn't* you?! Aaaahhhhhh..."
My aunt's machine gun–like delivery ended with a rapid descent to the ground.
Shouts along the lines of "What was that?!" and "I heard screaming!" echoed out from inside.
Awful. Absolutely awful.
"Hey, who's that lady?"
Instead of answering the short-haired girl's question, I hurriedly attempted to find a solution to this dilemma, sweat pouring down my brow.
In an instant, I thought up both the most innovative and the most painful of potential methods. It was the only way. The only way I had left. I grabbed the girl by the shoulders and attempted a friendly grin.

"Listen, can you punch me as hard as you can, like, right now?!"

"…Uh?"

The girl's face rewound back to the hostility she originally greeted me with, her eyes throwing a baneful glare at me. It didn't matter to me. I had to get back to normal, and I had to do it now.

The shouting grew louder inside, accompanied by footsteps. "Hey!" one of them said. "There's someone collapsed on the floor out there!"

"Please! I mean it! Don't hold anything back! Just punch me right now! Please!!"

The short-haired girl's face was a stone mask of disbelief. No more smiles from her now.

But I didn't care. I lightly shook her by the shoulders, and that was enough for her face to transform instantly.

The next moment, she gave me a look of naked, murderous rage.

Farewell, Friend Number One. It wasn't for long, but it was really fulfilling.

A sharp *smack!* echoed against the building walls.

It was a moment to remember—the very first of what'd turn out to be the many, many times Kido punched me.

The pale-orange light from the ceiling shone dolefully on the room and its tidily organized contents.

Which sounds like a good thing, but that cleanliness happened mainly because the room was almost devoid of possessions.

There was a small flat-screen TV, a low table with a checker pattern, a few pillow seats around it, and several children's books on a shelf.

Otherwise, it was flat and inorganic, decorated with little else but a couple of plain shelving units with our clothes and so on.

Room 107, the far end of the dormitory rooms on the ground floor.

On top of my dingy bed, the bottom bunk of one of the room's two bunk beds, we were engaged in yet another uncomfortable postmortem session.

The theme of today's meeting: how to deal with our reputation around the facility as "monsters."

Of course, yesterday's theme was on the same topic, and if you wanted to press the issue, it was the same thing the day before that, too.

Today, as well, I didn't get any particular feedback from the other two participants. There was no answer when I asked them what they were thinking about, and we had already spent the past two minutes under the dim light in silence.

Unable to withstand the silence any longer, I spoke up again. "Yeah, uh…Heh-heh-heh. What should we do, huh? Really."

I made every intention of inserting the nuance of "We're screwed" into that. Seto, in response, clutched the pillow in his hands even harder, looking ready to bawl at any moment.

"This is really all my fault. I'm so sorry..."

Kido immediately stepped up to cut off the mealy-mouthed Seto.

"No, no, it's not just your fault, Seto. We're not here to assign blame on people. Also, stop apologizing."

Seto shuddered for a moment, then buried his face into the pillow like he wanted to disappear, muttering "I'm sor...I mean, I'm not" into it.

Seto was always like that. Always ready to cry. Kind of like a cross between a small animal and a baby.

He cried when he tripped and fell, he cried when he was hungry, he cried when the sun set, and he cried even when nothing in particular happened to him.

That was the main identifying characteristic of Kousuke Seto, also known in my own mind as New Friend Number Two.

One would think it best to approach Seto with kid gloves when talking to him, but Kido never had any time for that.

"Huh," she gruffly replied as she started constructing a miniature Tokyo Tower string figure in her hands.

It felt a little cruel to just leave it at that, so I hurriedly tried to intervene.

"Listen, it's fine. Really. Seto, I know you're trying to seriously think about us and everything, so..."

"...Um, I'm sorry, but I'm really not thinking that much."

His muttered response through the pillow put an end to my noble attempt at comforting him.

"What did I just *tell* you?" Kido said, adding to the pressure. This made Kido twitch once again and fall into silence. Back to square one we went.

I sighed deeply and leaned back into the comforter I had propped against the wall.

We wouldn't make much progress today, either. I could already tell that this conference would end with all of us falling asleep sooner or later.

It had already been several months since I came here. The days were, shall we say, quite a lot more eventful than the two months or so I spent at my aunt's place. I wasn't sure how things would work out on that first day, when I acquired a nice crimson-red bruise on my cheek. But, thankfully, I've managed to keep a roof above my head here so far.

I was pretty surprised when I learned that Kido, the girl responsible for that bruise, was an orphan brought here for pretty much the same reason as myself. What's more, we wound up being assigned to the same room, which was a further shock to me.

Room assignments usually weren't coed like that, but since the other rooms were full and we were among the youngest residents, they made an exception for us.

I'd heard stories about how some people were just destined to meet each other, but this was the first time I'd actually felt it.

The name "Kido," by the way, also dates back to that first day, where she only got her last name out before I grabbed her and made her think I was some kind of weird predator. For a time afterward, she didn't even speak to me.

I kept hounding her after that, not wanting to lose Friend Number One so soon after making it. When she finally told me, "Stop breathing down my neck all day," I thought I was going to break into tears of joy. It took another month before she finally told me her first name, so I stuck to calling her Kido.

Lying in wait for the two of us in this room was Seto, the original occupant.

Seto was a quiet child—in a more literal way, not like Kido and her eternally crabby moods. But, perhaps in order to cheer me up while Kido continued to ignore me, he began to open up after a little while, and we started to chat about all kinds of things.

As he put it, he had been in this facility since right after he was born.

He had no friends, to the point where he was bullied by his previous roommates.

His only real companion, a dog named Hanako, died last year…and so on. All these tales, usually told through tears, didn't exactly cheer me up much.

But, as I attempted to calm him down with repeated assurances of "It's all right, it's all right," I suppose Seto and I managed to establish what you could call a "bond" with each other.

I guess that made our relationship much more friendshiplike than what I had with Friend Number One, who never even spoke to me.

That was about when Seto officially became Friend Number Two in my mind.

It wasn't because of the way that, when he asked me, "I guess we're friends now, right?" his eyes were giving me the message, "If you say no, I'm gonna die."

It purely came down to the fact that I found the time I spent with him to be…fun.

And as more time passed and Kido gradually began joining the conversation as well, the three of us began to get along like old friends. A few awkward patches here and there, but…

…Okay, a *lot* of awkward patches.

In fact, more hitches than nonhitches, really.

If this bed we lay on were a boat, it'd be one with the sails torn apart, the mast smashed to splinters, and a massive tidal wave menacing fifty feet in the air behind it.

Which is why we were having this postmortem.

To be frank, having residents in the other rooms—the facility staff, too—call us monsters and freaks all day was really starting to wear thin on us.

I was sick of going to Room 107 and seeing a Post-it with MONSTER HOUSE written on it stuck to the door. We had to do something to improve our image, the sooner the better.

M-monsters...Freaks...

"Hey, uh, I really wish you'd stop that...Wait, huh?"

I didn't say monster or freak out loud just now. All I did was think the words in my mind.

Why did he react to that? How was he able to?

I sat up and looked toward Seto. He, in turn, lifted his face from the pillow and returned the gaze with a teary-eyed one of his own.

Both of them were tinted a bright, mesmerizing shade of crimson.

After a pause, I said, "Oh," and closed my eyes, thinking a little.

(...Can you hear what I'm thinking again?)

I focused on the question in my mind.

"S-sorry. Yeah."

He sounded remorseful about it, burying his face once more into the pillow—just low enough so his eyes popped out above it.

So that's what it was.

(That hasn't happened so much lately,) I thought. *(Crazy how that always just happens to you out of the blue, Seto.)*

He lifted his head up slightly, mouth still covered. "I think it'll go away in a little bit," he said apologetically.

*   *   *

As I grinned at his reply, I felt Kido shifting positions on the bed. Fearing the worst, I gingerly turned toward her. She was staring at Seto like she couldn't stand another moment of breathing the same air as him.

I then shifted my gaze to Seto. He looked like a mouse caught in the sights of a cobra.

He waved his hands wildly in the air. "Ahhh!" he said, presumably in reply to her own internal voice. "I'm sorry! I didn't mean to apologize like…Huh? N-no! No, I'm not doing it on purpose!"

That habit couldn't have been more deep-rooted within him.

Kido, in response, unwound the cat's cradle she was working on. "How many times do I have to *tell* you," she said as she got on her knees, made a fist with her right hand, and began drawing near Seto.

The terror was too much for him to bear. He began sobbing on the spot, pathetically whining "Ahhh…! Ahhh…!" as he did.

It was probably time for me to do something.

I cut in between Seto and Kido, arms outstretched toward the latter.

"Whoa! Stop, stop, stop! Kido, you're getting a little too angry, all right?"

I tried giving her as natural a smile as I could (if a little strained) as I said it, but Kido glared at me instead, as if to say, "I'll kill you, too, if you don't move."

The way this girl stares at you…It really gets *to you.* If she had a role in a kids' action-rangers-style show, she'd definitely play a villain.

"Ha-ha," Seto said behind me. "Yeah, a villain."

(What're you laughing about?! I'm literally putting my body on the line against Kido for you!)

"I-I'm sorry!" Seto yelped.

Seto could be so careless like that. Now was absolutely *not* the time to start apologizing again. The aura of rage surrounding Kido grew noticeably more intense before my eyes.

"Not *again*…And you *said* something to him just now, didn't you, Kano?"

Her voice was soft, but every syllable had a dagger looming behind it.

"H-huh?! What do you mean? I didn't say anything! Did I, Seto?"

"N-no! No! He didn't call you a villain or anything!"

At the next instant, Kido landed a well-aimed body blow to my solar plexus.

"Gennhh!"

I was slammed down into the bedsheets. It was a perfectly clean knockout. I could hear a bell ringing somewhere.

"Hyaahh!" Seto pathetically shouted.

Withstanding the pain from my stomach, I groggily looked up toward Kido…only to find her sobbing, too. She must've crashed down from the apex of her anger.

As if reacting to it, Seto, naturally, began crying, too.

Now, as I stayed down for the count, I was surrounded by a stereo symphony of wailing.

…What is with *us tonight?*

Shouldn't I be the one who's crying here?

Amid my conflicting feelings, the sobbing that surrounded me began to ratchet up in volume.

"Oh, crap, if I don't…"

Suddenly realizing something, I turned to Kido. Just as I thought, her eyes gradually reddened as she began to disappear into nothingness before me.

*   *   *

For whatever reason, whenever Kido was angry, crying, lonely, or otherwise stressed, she would literally vanish…or, as she put it, other people would stop picking up on her presence. Assuming you don't actually touch her, though—otherwise, you'd see her again. That condition didn't make much sense to me, but there you go.

It was one thing if you could grab her hand or feel around in the air for her in time, but if she left the room in that invisible state, that was serious trouble.

She did that more than once in the past—so taken by whatever mood made her invisible that she just had to flee somewhere else. Seto and I had to spend hours searching for her during one episode, and as shameful as it was, I cried so hard then that I made Seto look like an amateur.

In the end, we searched until morning to no avail, only to return to our room and find Kido sleeping like a baby in her bed. So it worked out, but it wasn't an experience I wanted to repeat anytime soon.

If I didn't step up to put an end to this crying jag, I could have some serious clean-up work to do afterward.

So I conjured up an image in my mind. Another weapon in my arsenal, one I hadn't shown either of them yet. The shape, the voice, the scent…

The moment I opened my eyes, both of them cried out loud in unison. Just the reaction I was hoping for. I felt oddly proud of myself as I jumped down to the floor and waved at them.

They were both shocked at first, but as I beckoned, their tear-stained faces instantly transformed into bubbly smiles.

"You can do a *cat*?"

*   *   *

I could. Just for such an occasion, I had been spending my free time observing the strays around the facility in an attempt to memorize everything I could about them.

In the several months we knew each other, I discovered that Seto liked animals and Kido enjoyed cute things in general. Thus, I concluded that a black cat would be the perfect thing to distract both of them at once.

And it worked. Immediately, all their attention was focused on me.

Kido sat up out of bed, her breathing a bit ragged as she clapped her hands at me. "C'mere!" she said. "Come on, kitty, come 'ere!" Seto joined her, motioning at me with both hands.

The crimson quickly drained from their eyes as I watched. Kido finally, blessedly came back into full view.

Hee-hee-hee. Cute of her.

I bet she'd just love for me to jump into her lap. But let's string this out a little more.

I gingerly began to approach her, then suddenly reared back and kept my distance. I then repeated this a few times. Revenge was mine.

The mood of my audience swung from one extreme to the other every time I went through the cycle. They began attempting more and more flamboyant ways to curry my favor.

This was glorious. I was having so much fun, I could barely keep myself from rolling on my side and laughing. There was no stopping me now.

So, what next? How about a little dance? Yeah, that sounded nice.

Stepping up the intensity a bit, I hopped up on the table and began to bop around on two legs a bit. My audience grabbed their stomachs and howled in laughter.

So *much fun. This is the most fun night I've had in ages.*

It's been a long time since I've felt this good, actually. So this is what being a cat was like. I dug it. It might become a bad habit of mine.

As I continued doing a jig on the table, I heard an unexpected *whump* from nearby the door.

I didn't appreciate this interruption very much, but since the blood was quickly draining from the faces of my audience, I finally turned around for a look.

All the laughter made me fail to notice, but somewhere along the line, the door had been opened.

Right at the frame between our room and the hallway, one of the staffers—out on night patrol, probably—was lying on the floor.

I had trouble parsing the situation at first. What was this guy doing, all crumpled up on our doorstep? After another moment, though, it was clear as day.

Putting a halt to my performance, I felt my blood chill to freezing from head to claw.

"Uh…Hey, cat, what're we…?"

Even Kido was being uncharacteristically hesitant.

"Meow," I replied. That was the question I wanted to ask her, really. I sure as hell didn't have any bright ideas.

…The story, as I heard it later, was that as the staffer was doing his night rounds, he heard loud noises coming from Room 107, opened the door to warn the occupants, then claimed he saw a black cat hip-hop dancing on the table. The experience caused him to have a nervous breakdown, and he wound up being transferred to another facility.

This did nothing to improve our reputation, of course. In fact, it pretty much solidified Room 107's alternate name of Monster House for all time. Oh well.

*

So here we were once more, Room 107 at the far end of the first-floor dormitory hall.

On top of my dingy bed, the bottom bunk of one of the room's two bunk bed setups, we were engaged in yet another mind-achingly uncomfortable postmortem session.

The theme of today's meeting: "We're now officially 'monsters' in the eyes of this facility...and if this keeps up, we're screwed."

It was frightening, actually, this string of bad luck we were dealing with.

In fact, our reputation was getting worse and worse every day. From every corner of the building, all sorts of rumors were beginning to fly around about us.

One example:

"Every night, at the stall farthest away from the door in the first-floor girls' room, you can hear a ghostly voice sobbing to itself. No matter how hard you look, you'll never find anyone... but the voice is still there."

Apparently, this ghost made frequent visits to our room, as the prevailing theory went. I have no idea how the story got started. I mean, frequent visits? She *lives* here, dude.

I tried broaching the subject delicately with Kido. "I'm gonna punch whoever started that," came the aggravated reply. Guess it rang a bell with her. I refrained from further questioning.

Here's another one:

"One of the kids from Room 107 whispered something to a staffer, and then the guy disappeared the next day. Maybe it's the son of the Devil!"

I had no clue what could've been the seed for that tall tale. At first.

"Actually," Seto then said, "there was this one guy who was going around wearing girls' underwear under his uniform, and I told him, 'You shouldn't be doing that,' and then I never saw him again."

Well, chalk that one up to us as well, I suppose.

Why was the staffer doing something like that? Why did he stop coming to the facility afterward? How could we have known? We were all still too young for all that.

How about one more to make it a solid trio?:

There was another story about "some guy who hangs out behind the dorms and keeps sniffing at stray cats." Yes, that was me. I wanted to die when I heard that one.

These dark rumors about us seemed to inflate and exaggerate themselves on a daily basis. It was like a never-ending merry-go-round for me.

Not for the other two. They never cared very much about the rest of society, anyway, it seemed like. Just me.

Now I was in the middle of relaying a few of these latest rumors about us to them, ending each one with, "So what do you guys think?"

"I think you're a freak, Kano."

Kido's eyes unwaveringly bore down on me.

"Huh? Uhhh…Huh?"

The answer was merciless as it was to the point. It came so suddenly that I thought she was making some kind of metaphor at first.

"I said you're a freak."

All right. Not a metaphor, then. I tried my best to withstand the barrage, driving the topic back toward our traction session.

"No, I…I wasn't asking you what you thought about me picking up cats and sniffing at them. I'm talking about what we should do about…this…"

"Hraa-a-a-aahh…"

Kido, breathlessly disinterested in my attempt, yawned.

I could feel the tears coming.

Why do I have to sit here and have people call me a freak on my own bed? I'm trying to make things better for us.

"You aren't a freak at all," Seto whispered into my ear, perhaps picking up on my despair. "I do it a lot, too."

…I'm sorry if this sounds mean, Seto, but at least I had a half-decent reason.

"Hey, so how long're we gonna do this, anyway?"

Kido rubbed her eyes, her voice betraying her intense fatigue. "I mean, is there any point to it?"

"Um…Well, uh, you know…"

I didn't exactly have a good reply to that question. I invited the two of them over here virtually every night for these "postmortems," but up to now, there wasn't even a whiff of an idea, much less an ace in the hole that would completely turn our reputations around and make life more decent for us.

"…I mean, if things keep going like this around here, they might, like, seriously kick us out of here, wouldn't they?"

"Th-they're gonna kick us out?!"

My observation made Seto almost leap out of his position on the bed. I began to wonder what kind of mutant tear ducts he had in order to mass produce so much of the stuff on a moment's notice.

"Ugh, no crying, okay? No crying."

"I'm sorry…"

He nodded and wiped them away as I rubbed his back. He

had a knack for turning off the waterworks at a moment's notice—one of his saving graces. *Still cries too much, though.*

"I mean, I don't think they're gonna boot us out to the street tomorrow or anything. But I think some of the staff's starting to get scared of us, so if we don't make an effort to be more likable pretty soon..."

"Likable...?"

Not that there was any plan of action I could think of. Was it even possible, really, to raise our likability level from the bottomless pit it was hurtling down right now?

I didn't think there was much way we could be branded anything worse than "monsters." But now that we were this far down, how were we ever gonna claw our way back up to "humans"?

"...Pfft. She's sleeping."

As I worried away to myself, Kido began lightly snoring, still sitting primly on her side of my bed. Aha. That would explain why she didn't lunge at Seto for apologizing earlier.

Not much purpose waking her up. That'd just rile her up again. I placed a hand on Kido's back and carefully laid her down on my bed.

"She's really not that freaky a girl, though," I said, giving her a light tap on the cheek. "Not as much as people think."

"If she doesn't get angry," Seto added, giggling to himself.

"Nhh," Kido said in her sleep.

"Eeeee!!" Seto shouted, tumbling backward.

If I could show these two people right now to the rest of the kids, they'd probably feel pretty stupid, freaking out so much over just a bunch of dumb children. But I didn't have it in me to assert this in front of them strongly enough. Unless I interacted with people more—unless I talked to them more—they'd never learn the truth. They needed to if we were gonna get anywhere, but that was hard for us. It was hard, but if we could get them on our side, maybe we could all get along, then.

The problem, though…

"It's these 'eyes,' aren't they? Our problem."

Seto sat back up from his sprawled position on the bed. His eyes had morphed into blood red somewhere back there.

"I'm sorry, I kind of heard you a little again."

I chuckled a little. *(This is better anyway,)* I thought. *(Now we won't wake up Kido.)*

"If you like," Seto replied with a contented smile.

(What is with these powers, though? I mean, for real. Are they some kind of occult superpowers, like on TV shows and stuff?)

"Ugh. That…? I dunno, I think we should probably ask someone…"

Tears began to well into Seto's eyes.

(Ha-ha-ha! Never mind, never mind. But we can't really go blabbing about this to everyone, you know?)

"I—I guess not…I'm too scared."

We had gone over this topic in previous postmortems—people thought we were "monsters" because, quite frankly, we had some pretty inhuman powers.

All we knew about our own abilities came from our attempts to harness them. We certainly weren't experts, and while I couldn't speak about myself, I knew that Seto and Kido still had trouble fully controlling their powers.

If we all could, that'd probably cut the bad rumors by at least half or so.

We had also considered speaking with a grown-up, of course. But a drama on TV we happened to be watching quashed that idea pretty quickly.

By sheer coincidence, the show starred a guy called a "psychometrer" who could read people's minds. We laughed about it at first—"Hey, Seto, they did a biopic of you!"—but then he was captured by some terror group, subjected to hideous experiments, and ultimately died.

Our expressions then, especially Seto's, made us look like someone had stashed us in the freezer for a few hours: "People with powers like ours get experimented upon and killed." It said so on TV, so it had to be true.

Several minutes later, Seto began shaking, crept into his bunk, and didn't come out again for another twenty-four hours.

The word "psychometrer" was forbidden around Seto from that point forward. Kido had taken the habit of using it like a magic word, whispering it into Seto's ear now and again to see how he'd react.

So, for now at least, our three powers were still a secret that never ventured beyond this room.

(I'm sure you are, but...I mean, we have no idea where these powers came from. We don't know what they mean. I think that's a lot scarier.)

"That's true, yeah. Mine and Kido's just kind of come out at random, so..."

Seto sighed. His power to read what people were thinking seemed to vary in length and strength from instance to instance. When it came in strong enough, he claimed, he could even read people's feelings and past memories.

On the other hand, during sudden little jags like this one, the best he could hope for was to pick up on words his target consciously thought of in his brain.

Seto explained all of that to us in simple terms once. But unless you're the one experiencing it, a lot of the logic behind it didn't make much sense to us.

(Yeah, that's really a drag. With Kido in particular, you can spot her right out when it's happening.)

She had it more under control than what she had to deal with a while ago, but Kido still wasn't in full grasp of her "invisibility" powers.

The way she put it, it happened whenever something "ticked her off." That didn't sound very scientific, but we had nothing else to go on.

Fortunately, it hadn't resulted in any serious disasters...or I'd like to believe it hadn't, at least. She really needed to learn how to harness it before things got even worse for us, though.

There had to be *some* kind of trick, right?

"It'd be nice if I could at least, like, keep it from triggering..."

(Keep it from triggering, huh? I think we need to keep you from crying all the time first, Seto.)

I grinned at Seto. He blushed. "Yeah."

(But all joking aside, that might actually be related. You and Kido, your powers never come out much when you aren't crying, right?)

"B-but I don't how much I can do about—I mean, I'm trying to change, but it's kind of hard to..."

Seto shrugged at me, crestfallen.

(And you keep apologizing, too.)

"Ngh...Yeah. Sorry."

Then he looked even more crestfallen. Clearly, he wasn't doing that on purpose. I'm sure Kido knew that, too, but she never let up on him on that score.

It was strange. Something about the general lack of control they had over their powers—their emotions, really—made me feel really well put together by comparison.

Though, really, that extended to every other kid in this building. They all seemed kind of awkward, blundering their way through life, and they always had to me. I felt like my powers gave me an insider's view of how people grow and mature as human beings, and I hated myself a lot for it.

"But I gotta admit, Kano, I really look up to you. You can use your ability at will like it's nothing. You're always trying to help us out, too."

Seto smiled as he said it, but something about the glowing review failed to cheer me up.

(Huh? Oh, I do not! I'm exactly the same as you guys. There's a ton I don't get about this, and everything's just as scary for me, so...)

"...Oh?"

I'm presuming the words I pictured came through to him loud and clear, but they seemed to throw Seto off a bit. He tilted his head at me, and as I looked up to meet his gaze, I found that his eyes were back to normal, not a hint of red to them.

"...Oh! I think it's died down! Whew...Sorry I keep putting you through this."

He bowed his head at me a few times in apology. I formed a smile on my face.

"Mm? Ahh, don't worry about it! It's really not a big deal at all."

"But that last thing you thought right then, Kano...I, I don't think I got it fully..."

"...Oh! Is that it? Guess you lost your power too fast to catch it all, huh? Maybe that mixed up a few wires in your brain."

"M-maybe," Seto said, shoulders drooping down. "Oof...It just comes and goes as it pleases, you know? It's really mean to me."

"Yeah...Well, it's cool. Besides, it's kind of fun, Seto...Watching your power mess around with you like that."

I was only half-joking.

"Oh, stop picking on me like that," he replied, cheeks puffed out. "I really need to work on changing that! It's hard for me to keep causing trouble for all of you like this, so..."

His limp-wristedness was gone now. In its place was what

seemed to be genuine resolve, something I hoped I could count on someday.

"Hee-hee! Well, no need to rush it. Take your time. You don't have to try and force yourself to—"

"Yes, he does."

Kido interrupted me midsentence.

That innocent cuteness she demonstrated while asleep was gone. Now her face was back to her usual sharp, be-fanged self as she glared at Seto.

"Are you *ever* gonna stop apologizing?" she whispered.

"Eep," Seto replied weakly. I should have been used to this exchange by now, but this time, it really annoyed me for some reason. I couldn't help but speak up.

"...Hey, you don't have to be like that, okay?"

Kido, not bothering to move, shifted her eyes from Seto to me. "Like what?" she said as she began to sit up.

Normally, at a time like this, I'd try to defuse the situation with a laugh. Right now, I couldn't. This was getting too frustrating.

"Well, didn't you hear Seto? He's trying to change, you know."

"Yeah," she spat out, "but he *isn't*. I tell him over and over again..."

Not willing to bend an inch, was she?

"Umm..."

Seto attempted to interject. But there was no stopping me now.

"...You know, you're really pissing me off."

I should have just shut up, but I couldn't. I had to give her the truth. And I was gaining momentum.

"You never think about other people's feelings. All you think about every day is yourself. Like, who do you think you are? 'Cause I'm seriously having trouble putting up with that act any longer. Besides, Kido, you're—"

Once I reached that point, I felt a violent shock to the right side of my face, my vision blurring.

It came so suddenly that my brain shut off for a moment. But, hearing Seto's silent scream next to me, I finally realized that Kido just gave me a full-palm slap.

"Ow..."

I glared at Kido. Something dark and ugly within me welled up from parts unknown, filling my heart to the brim.

Kido must have been the same way. A snarl of hostility erupted across her face.

"Who's the one not thinking about other people's feelings here, huh? You have no idea what I'm going through at *all*."

Kido's eyes were glowing redder and redder by the moment. As if on cue, the right hand she used to brutally slap me began to fade into the background. I'd seen that unfold dozens of times before, but tonight I was out of words to comfort her with.

"Ha! How should I know? You're too busy beating the crap out of me all the time to say. I'm not Seto, you know. And, what, you're disappearing on me again? Man, good thing you got that get-out-of-jail-free card whenever someone actually calls you out on your crap, huh?"

I probably could have phrased it more eloquently, but I meant what I said. I wanted to knock her down a peg, and my emotions were running at full capacity.

Kido was awestruck for a moment. Then her face reddened like a tomato. Then she grabbed me.

"You goddamn...!"

I fell back, unable to bear the full brunt of her weight.

Struggling, I tried to push her off, but I failed to turn the tables on her. Pathetic, I know, but Kido had me completely outclassed physically.

Now fully on top of me, Kido laid another full-force slap on my head. The sharpness of it made Seto eject a powerless whimper.

"Oww…What's with you? You're just trying to—"

"Shut *up*! Stop talking!"

Kido covered my mouth with both hands. Unable to speak, I began kicking my legs into the air as I moaned and groaned at her. The tears from her eyes dropped down onto my own reddened cheeks.

"I…I *hate* you, Kano!"

The statement made my heart writhe in pain. I couldn't even summon the energy to whip my legs around anymore.

Now I was experiencing a dull, cold pain, different from the burning I felt when she slapped me. It was like someone forced me to swallow an ice cube. That pain, engineered by Kido's words, bound my heart tighter and tighter the more I comprehended what they meant.

The emotion from both of us was to the point that, once I finally brushed Kido's hands off my head, she brought them up to her own face and started to sob.

I had no words for her as Kido broke down in front of me.

What should I say? Now that she said she hated me, what else would she want from me? As my brain scrambled for a killer comeback, a pair of unexpected words wandered out from my lips.

"…Yeah, great."

The statement left me intensely bewildered. I had no intention of saying anything like that. Why did *that* come out?

I looked at Kido. Her expression showed her dismay, telling me that I just did something I could never take back.

To be honest, I would've preferred it if she just slapped me again, as per usual.

If that helped her settle down—if that kept her from hating me—I wouldn't mind being scarred from head to toe as a result.

But Kido made no move. Wiping the tears with her right hand, she got up off of me and moved away from my bed.

"W-wait a sec, Kido! I'm s—"

"...It's fine. Don't talk to me."

She didn't even turn around as she replied. I was still in shock over the coldness of it all when Seto joined her off the bed, shouting, "I'm sorry! This is all my fault!" as he did. He then covered his mouth in a panic. *Oops. Did it again.* His constant clumsiness was even starting to get on *my* nerves.

But Kido didn't bother to reproach him for it this time. "It's *fine*, Seto," she quietly replied. "Also, I'm leaving."

Seto and I froze.

"Wh-what are you—?"

"I had a meeting with the superintendent. He said there's someone willing to take me in...I was thinking I'd say no, but I think I'll go after all."

It was all so sudden, it left me feeling faint. It made too much sense to be a joke, and Kido never told jokes, anyway. Plus, I knew Seto would pinch-hit for me in a moment.

"Y-you're kidding, right?! I'm sorry..."

There we go. At least it was enough to make Kido turn toward us again.

"I'm not. Also, you *have* to...ahh, never mind."

She looked a tad repentant for a moment, but quickly turned her heels and burrowed herself into her bunk. "The next time you talk to me," she said, "I'll hit you for *real*." Then she fell silent.

Those weren't "for real" just now?

...Silence reigned for a while.

Seto and I stared at Kido's bed, not even bothering to exchange glances with each other. In an extremely rare showing for Seto, he wasn't crying. It didn't seem like he was bottling anything up, either. The shock of it all must have fried his brain circuits.

I wasn't one to talk, either. My own brain felt like a bowl full of mush.

Being told that she hated me and to not talk to her left me with pretty much nothing to work with.

Kido must have known that. That was why she took that strategy. If you wanted someone you "hate" out of your life, that was a pretty effective way to do it.

"What's gonna happen to us now...?"

"...I dunno."

There was little else I could give to Seto's sudden question. I lay down on my bed and closed my eyes. If I didn't, I felt like I'd wind up taking my anger out on Seto instead.

Seto attempted a few "ums..." and "heys" after that. But, realizing I was done for the night, he gave a final "I'm really sorry about this" and climbed up to the top bunk.

I heard sobs from above me a little while later, but it wasn't too long before the room was silent again.

My mind ran over a few theories, a few possibilities in the quiet. A few memories, too. But I wasn't about to discover a miracle method that'd bring back the fun times we had up to yesterday, and sooner or later, I fell asleep.

Kido's adoptive parents came over exactly a week later. For the whole seven days, she never spoke to us.

*

"Wow, this weather's really great! It makes me wanna go out on a picnic or something!"

A jovial voice popped up from the driver's seat, attempting to break through the oppressive environment inside the car.

Seated directly behind the driver, I just responded with a light sigh.

It wasn't that I was setting out to be rude.

The people walking up and the down the sidewalks we drove past all had heavy coats on. Things looked brutal out there. If we really wanted to load up the picnic basket and head to the park right now, both our food and ourselves would freeze to death within the hour.

But I didn't want to act all contrarian, either. The kid who didn't know how to act around others. That'd make things seriously rough for me.

So, corking all of those thoughts up, I just sighed.

Seto, unable to take the silence in the front passenger seat, chuckled a little.

"But…but don't you think it's a little cold for a picnic?"

I was afraid he was reading my mind again, but the color of his eyes indicated otherwise.

"Oh, no way! You guys're all kids—you can deal with a little bit of nippiness to the air. Right? We can get everything packed up once we're home!"

The driver sounded as blissfully carefree as always.

"Ah-ha-hah…"

Seto must've not had any better response at the ready.

Despite his personality, Seto liked to spend a surprisingly large amount of time outdoors.

He'd regularly go out by himself, only to come back with his clothes all dirty after chasing forest animals around or whatever.

Even a month ago, he spent the entire winter's day outdoors while I was curled into a ball in my room, attempting to keep icicles from forming on me.

So his take just now didn't make sense.

Having him suggest that it was too cold to go outside was absolutely unnatural for him. But I couldn't blame him for his little white lie, either. After all, we couldn't have been in a worse social situation right now.

I took a quick glance to my left. My eyes met with Kido's as she sat there. She immediately grumped at me and turned her eyes away, toward the window. I was hoping for a little more when we locked eyes, but I shrugged in resignation (and more than a bit of anger) and turned toward my own window.

The two of us had been like this since our fight at last week's postmortem.

Living in the same room, we couldn't help but look at each other now and again. But despite how hard it was to keep a grudge going in our circumstances, we still adamantly refused to talk to each other.

Seto acted like he was in a panic the whole time, but—maybe because he realized anything he'd do would just make it worse—he didn't comment about it much.

Not that I didn't want to talk to Kido. In fact, I tried to make peace with her in my own way, in an effort to mend things as soon as possible. But whenever I made any kind of move toward her, she'd glare at me and refuse any of my advances.

She told me not to talk to her, so there wasn't much else I could do. The days of agonizing over it in my mind continued.

"But hey, um, sorry about the suddenness and all, you know? I guess maybe the superintendent didn't tell you we were adopting all three of you?"

That was the thing about it. The sudden and completely unexpected thing.

It turns out that the Tateyamas, the family that agreed to take Kido, had actually meant to adopt all three of us from the start.

Seto and I hadn't heard anything about that, of course. We were completely in the dark about it until the superintendent called us in two days ago.

I didn't think this could happen—not meeting the family beforehand, not being brought into the loop at all, just, "Okay, your new family's coming over in a couple days." Whether they saw us more as monsters than children by now or not, that was just cruel.

They must have appreciated the chance to get rid of all three of us menaces at once, but the complete lack of compassion behind it honestly peeved me.

But we couldn't refuse them, of course. Seto and I had to jump on the opportunity before there was any chance we'd miss it.

We sure didn't have any lingering affection for the facility, anyway. It was nothing but grudges, from start to finish.

For both of us, depressed over the fact that Kido was off someplace far away without so much as another word, this was an opportunity beyond our wildest dreams.

*　　*　　*

"No, but, uh…Hey, this is great! Getting to join you as a family and all…We couldn't be any happier!"

Seto turned to the backseat.

"R-right, guys?"

Why're you turning toward us, *you dumbass,* I thought to myself. Sadly, Seto's eyes weren't red, and "Please, just say yes" was written across his face. "Yeah, it's really great," I reluctantly agreed.

"Yehh…" was the vague response from the peeved-looking Kido.

Seto began to quiver a little, the awkward smile still on his face, which all but screamed to me, "If you could just act a *little* nicer…"

It wasn't that Seto had finally gained control over his ability. It was just that his facial expressions were too easy to read.

But while Kido was still clearly peeved, she didn't act particularly unhappy upon learning we were coming along for the ride.

I was sweating it out for a while, wondering if she'd refuse to go once she found out we were joining her. I suppose we had nothing to worry about on that front, but judging by her demeanor, she sure hadn't forgiven me yet. That unnerved me.

Are we ever going to patch things up, where we're going?

"Okay, here we are! Hop on out, kids!"

The car stopped inside the lot, and as we filed out, we were greeted by a small red brick house. Seto and I stood there for a bit, examining its unfamiliar contours. For a residential neighborhood, it stuck out. I bet Seto was wondering if this kind of thing was normal in this town.

"…Cute."

Kido blurted out the appraisal.

I turned around. Kido, noticing this, blushed and glared at me with her best "What are you looking at, you pile of garbage?" leer. I thought about saying something in self-defense, but "The next time you talk to me, I'll hit you for *real*" ran across my mind just in the nick of time. I opted to stay mum.

But...Ah. Right. Kido did like cute things. A house like this probably ranked as "cute" in the eyes of most young girls.

And as I recalled this, an idea began to take shape.

Maybe Kido would like it if I turned into a cat again.

The last time I did, she was enthralled, completely forgetting that it was still "me" inside. I wonder why I never thought about that. Well, perfect, then. One more time around, and...

"Okay, kids, c'mon in!"

I walked in through the open door to find that, despite the unusual exterior, the inside was no different from the kind of typical family residence you'd see on TV all the time.

All the smells, nothing like what I had back when living in my own room, made me realize all the more that I was starting a new life.

"Hee-hee! What do you think of your new home? Feel free to use whatever you see lying around, okay? ...Oh, but I guess I better formally introduce myself. My name is Ayaka Tateyama. You can think of me as your mother, or as whatever else—anything's fine. But hopefully you'll be seeing all of us as family soon!"

Ayaka's smile as she said this cleanly washed away any concerns that remained in my heart.

"Th-thank you very much."

"Sure thing!" Ayaka replied, patting my head.

I looked toward Seto and Kido, a little embarrassed. They looked back at me, a little jealous.

"And you guys, too!" Ayaka said, quickly picking up on this and patting both of their heads. Her palms must have the power to calm people down or something. They both looked remarkably serene as they accepted the attention.

"Okay, then. Do you kids mind playing in your room until your big sister comes home?"

That made the two of them freeze in place. I followed their guide.

"S-sister...?" Seto anxiously asked.

"Hmm?" replied Ayaka. "Well, you'll have a sister who's a year older than you all, but...didn't the superintendent mention that?" She stopped, a confused look on her face.

I almost blurted out, "I'm sorry, that superintendent guy pretty much told me nothing," but Seto spoke up first.

"...Ohhh! Oh! Maybe so, yeah!"

I nodded silently. We'd been greeted with nothing but warmth and kindness so far. There was no point throwing stones at it or asking too many needless questions. If this sister person was Ayaka's daughter, I was sure she'd be just as kind and gentle to us.

Seto and I nodded our agreement to each other, confirming that we both shared the same opinion. It reminded me all over again how much of a bond we'd built over the past two months, on a constant vigil to keep Kido on our good side. I didn't exactly look back on it with fondness, but...

Kido, unaware of our thoughts, turned pale and began to shake a little.

"Hmm? Is something wrong? You all right?"

"N-no, I'm fine," Kido weakly replied. Clearly, she wasn't, something Ayaka spotted. "Are you worried about your sister, maybe?" she said, patting her head.

Surprisingly, this was enough to immediately soften Kido's expression as she let out a soft "no" in response. There must really be some kind of magic force hidden in her palm.

We were all still huddled just beyond the front door. It was time to explore the house a little more.

Going down the hall, we found a door just before the stairs with a sign reading Kids' Room printed on it.

"This is just for the time being, but I was thinking we'd use this for your room, starting today."

Ayaka opened the door, revealing a room far larger, and far more well lit by the sun, than the oppressive Room 107 we used to call home.

"Wow…"

Seto couldn't hide his amazement. His eyes began to sparkle as he imagined the future childhood he'd spend here.

We all swarmed into the room, each of us examining whatever took our interest. There was a closet packed with toys, a shelf lined with an oddly extensive line of superhero comics… Everything we discovered made us more and more excited.

"Well! Glad you guys seem to like it, I guess! Now play nice until your sister comes home, all right?"

With a final smile, Ayaka closed the door. The three of us were left alone in the children's room.

That, of course, left us to ponder over what this "sister" was really like.

The thought never occurred to us while Ayaka was around, but now that our first encounter was looming at any moment, it made us anxious.

I turned toward my two companions. They must've had the same concern. Each of them was seated, looking at the floor and fidgeting. Our tacit agreement meant that they couldn't just say "What next?" or whatever to each other. Not with Kido around, who publicly promised to hit the next person who spoke to her. Neither of us was willing to take that risk.

An awkward silence unfolded. *Do we really have what it takes to survive in this family?*

Seto began to steal glances at me. Probably counting on *me* to do something. Damn it. The silence and anxiety was making me restless.

"…I'm gonna go to the bathroom."

So I decided to leave the room. Seto flashed me a seething "Don't leave me alone with her!" glare as I shut the door. It broke my heart to, but I closed it anyway. "Hang in there, Seto!" I shouted in my mind. I didn't want to wait around for a reply, so I headed off in search of the john.

Heading down the hall a little ways, I spotted a door with w/c written on it in English letters. I didn't know any of the language back then, but even I knew what that sign meant.

I headed inside and heaved a sigh. I don't know why, but being in a bathroom alone always had a calming effect on me. Maybe, since I didn't have my own room, it was because bathrooms were the only place I could really be by myself.

The thought depressed me a little, but I decided not to dwell on it.

But what am I going to do now?

I wasn't about to stroll on back to the house of horrors I just left. But barricading myself in the bathroom for too long could make my new family worry about me.

What should I do?

"Hey, I'm home!"

Suddenly, a loud voice made itself easily heard through the bathroom door.

My heart thudded loudly in my ears.

Right after that, there was a clattering of footsteps and the unlatching of a door before things fell silent again.

It was easy to picture our "sister" at the front door from where I was standing.

Whoever it was sounded like a bright, energetic woman. Not the type to wheedle or backstab people.

Although—*Oh man, what if she is...?*

...Wait. What am I thinking? Haven't I just spent my entire life being judged and hated as a bad influence without any chance to defend myself? And here I was, trying to guess someone's personality from their voice alone. *I'm awful.*

There's no telling until I meet her myself. That's how relationships work.

"Right," I said to myself, and then I left the bathroom.

Judging by the noise I heard, our "sister" went right into the children's room after arriving home. That meant Kido and Seto already knew who their sister was going to be. I felt a bit nervous about that, but I knew them well enough—they might be too scared to say anything, but they weren't going to spout off nonsense or immediately shun her or anything.

In fact, maybe they were hitting it off great right now. *You never know,* I thought, as I approached the door.

With a deep breath, I brought a hand to the doorknob.

But just as I was about to push it open, I heard a mumbled "Gehh!" from the other side.

...Wait a second.

I've heard that before.

A pretty long time ago...at the park...

*   *   *

Once my mind reached that point, I finally realized the devastating truth and threw the door open.

Just as I thought, I was greeted by a girl curled into a ball on the floor, moaning to herself painfully.

"Ooooh…"

Kido, standing next to her, shifted her eyes from the fallen girl to me, muttering to herself. "H-how come you didn't turn back after I punched you…? How come there're two of you, Kano…?"

I immediately stampeded my way back to the bathroom, locked the door, and knelt on the floor.

"C'mon, God, that's not even fair…"

In fact, it was awful.

I knew there wasn't much point bitching at a God who I didn't know was around to listen or not, but I felt like I had a decent claim here.

Who could have predicted anything like this?

My "sister" was that girl I ran into at the park.

It was a preposterous coincidence. I was astonished things like this happened in the world. I wish I could meet whoever arranged this new torment for me. I'd definitely have a word or two for him.

If that was all there was to it, then all right. Hey, it's a small world, yeah?

But it wasn't. That girl definitely looked like she took one of Kido's full-strength body blows. Voice of experience talking here.

I imagined the girl practically flying into the room, beaming, going on like, "Here I am, guys! Your new sister!" That would be wholly expected behavior toward your new siblings, I supposed. In fact, it probably would've made me happy to see.

But, from Kido's perspective, that heartfelt welcome probably looked like a cruel joke on my part.

She was already waiting for her "sister" with bated breath, only to find the guy she was actively quarreling with busting open the door, transformed into that girl I always liked turning into, and spouting nonsense about how *I* was her sister.

Yeahhh...
"...*I'd* probably punch her, too."

My muttering to myself was drowned out by loud knocking on the door, followed by someone roughly jiggling the doorknob.

"Agghhh!"
I instinctively screamed.
"I know you're in there. Get out. Now."
The emotionless Kido's words sounded like "I'll kill you" repeated several times to me.
The first time she speaks to me in a week, and this is what I get. This world is so cruel.
"W-wait a sec! I got a stomachache..."
"Yeah, sure. Get out here and I'll make it all better, okay?"
"Ahhh...! P-please! Cut me some slack! How was I supposed to know *this* was gonna happen...?!"
I was pleading for my life. I couldn't have sounded any more pathetic.
Wham! The door shuddered, almost breaking at the impact of Kido's force.
Well, I thought, *no escaping from this. One punch like that, and I'm a goner. Time to pay the piper.* I gave up all hope and opened the door.

It went without saying that Kido was now the living personification of unharnessed, uncontrollable rage.

"Any last words?"

"...Okay, just let me say one mor—*ooof*!!"

Before she even gave me a chance to finish, she jackhammered her fist into my stomach. I instantly crumpled down to the bathroom floor.

...Why'd she even ask, then?

Ahh, my consciousness is fading away from me.

Once I'm gone, Seto, you'll need to stay strong. You can't let her get the best of you. Please!

"Hmm? Are you...?"

From far away, I could hear someone talking. I wondered who it was.

"Oh, it is! The kid I ran into at the park! Wow, small world, huh?!"

My near-extinguished consciousness was quickly whisked back to reality.

Fighting off the pain as I zoomed to my feet, I saw the girl on the ground earlier, looking down at me with a smile.

Her hair, medium in length, was as deeply black as her eyes. She was completely unchanged from when I last saw her.

"Good to see you again. Do you remember me at all?"

That form, that voice, that scent...Not a day passed by when I didn't recall it.

I promised we'd talk again tomorrow, and then I walked away, figuring that was the last of it. Now we were together again, in the last place I ever expected.

...And in the bathroom, no less. Insult to injury.

Kido brought a tentative hand to the girl's stomach, likely concerned about any permanent damage she did.

"Hmm? Oh, I'm fine! A-OK here! I got some muscle down there, so…"

She cleared her throat and jutted her chest forward for effect.

"It's gonna take a lot more than *that* to kill me, lemme tell ya! …But, boy, what a surprise! Punching me at first sight like that! That's a pretty killer secret move you got!"

She smiled and patted Kido's head.

"I'm sorry…It's all Kano's fault."

Kido looked a little ashamed as she stepped up and assigned me all the blame. The girl raised an eyebrow.

"Oh, yeah, you said that before. What's up with that?"

Squirming under the guilt, I felt obliged to state my case.

"N-no! No, she's lying to you! We can explain all of this…"

"You can? Ooh, I'd be interested to hear it!"

Uh-oh. Maybe I piqued her interest a little too much for my own good.

The girl peered into my eyes, a curious smile on her face.

Greeting her form, her voice, her scent with my five senses once again reminded me that this was the same girl who had lived in my mind all these years.

Come to think of it, why did this girl stay so vividly alive in my head after just a single encounter? It took me days before I finally got the hang of the whole cat thing.

I melted on the spot, machine-gunning out "uhs" and "ums" around the room.

But the girl didn't wait. "…But, uh, maybe later, then!" she said and gave me a gregarious smile.

"We should get to know each other's names first, anyway! How's that sound?"

The girl turned around and jogged back to our room.

Kido gave me a glance. "I haven't forgiven you, by the way," she spat at me as she followed the girl out. "You better explain this to me later."

So much for hoping these events softened her up a bit.

I waited for them to fully enter the room before I took a long, deep breath and followed them.

*

Once inside, I did what I could to assuage Seto.

"I thought she was going to kill me," he said through teary eyes. Luck was probably the only thing that saved him.

If anything had turned out differently, he might've been a dead man.

Following the girl's instructions, the three of us lined up in a row, facing her directly as she knelt on the ground.

"Okay, you ready?"

The girl was excited, as if waiting her whole life for this moment.

"My name's Ayano. Ayano Tateyama! But *you* can call me 'Big Sis,' all right?"

Ayaka made it clear earlier that we were free to call her whatever we wanted. By comparison, this girl, Ayano, wasn't taking no for an answer.

Kido followed.

"Um, my name's Tsubomi Kido. Good to meet you."

Next to her, Seto gave a look that resembled a pigeon shot with a BB gun. Not only was Kido being politely friendly in a way she had never been with us—she freely gave out her first

name, something we practically had to extract from her like it was her appendix. I couldn't blame him for being surprised.

I looked on, a bit miffed, trying my best to keep from commenting on this newfound tractability.

Seto continued on.

"Um, Kousuke Seto..."

He kept it short. I liked that.

At least he managed to get his entire name out in one go. From him, that's a stellar effort. The first time I met him, it took Seto a few hours to venture out from under his bedsheets, much less tell me his name. Compared to that, he was honestly making impressive progress.

Now I was up.

"My name's Shuuya Kano. Thanks a lot."

The girl nodded at each of us in order.

"Great! Now we all know each other's names."

"Y-yeah," I replied, facing downward to keep from showing her my blushing face.

The moment we finished with the self-intros, the girl began fidgeting to herself once again.

"All right, then! With that out of the way, it's about time you, uh..."

About time we do what?

Judging by the way she put it, it must've been something she planned in advance. But we had nothing to go on. We patiently awaited the resolution, only to have the wind taken right out of our sails.

"Could you maybe start calling me 'Big Sis' now?"

The girl glanced at me first.

"Or, on the other hand, regular old 'Sister' is fine, too...?"

Then she winked at me.

On the other hand: *What…?*

Right. So that's what she meant. She just wanted her newly minted younger brothers and sisters to make it official in her eyes.

Sneaking a look over, I found Seto staring blankly into space. Kido, meanwhile, appeared to be deeply pondering some question or another.

"All right," she said after a moment, "…Big Sis."

This seemed to instantly elate the girl. "Oooh, Tsubomi!" she said. "That's so cuuuute!" She gave Kido a loving pat on the shoulder, then whisked herself straight over to Seto and me.

Her twinkling eyes had "Okay, your turn next" written all over them. I could feel the waves of pressure pounding upon us.

"Wh-what's up? I'm your big sis, right? Come on…"

Her face, as it sidled ever closer to our own, was crisscrossed with sheer determination.

"B-Big Sis!"

Seto shouted it without hesitation.

I could tell he just wanted this over with, but the girl didn't seem to care. "All *right!*" she said as she patted his head. "That's the way to do it, Kousuke!"

It made Seto look remarkably happy.

That left me last.

The girl's eyes turned to mine, once again drawing dangerously close.

It would've been easy to just say it, of course. But it felt a little weird, the "big sis" stuff. I honestly thought this girl was either my age or maybe a year younger.

"Come onnn," she said, eyes locked with mine, wholly unaware of my hesitation. "What am I to you, hmm?"

All right. I give up, If that's what she wants, fine. It might feel weird, but once I get in the habit of saying it, it'll be done.

"Uh, Sis…?"

The moment I uttered the single most important syllable in her life, I felt the word tuck itself straight into some forgotten corner of my heart.

Simply saying it made my brain begin to identify the girl in front of me as my family.

The girl blinked in apparent surprise. "'Sis'…? Huh. I guess there was that, too, huh?"

I stared back at her. What was she *talking* about? But she once again paid me no mind.

"Well…okay! Sure! Great! Good to meet you, Shuuya," she said as she patted my head.

From that moment on, the girl in front of me was Sis. And being patted by her had a sort of…irritating feel to it. Much different from Ayaka. I was so embarrassed by it that I edged away from her.

My "sister" puffed up her cheeks. "You're trying to avoid me, aren't you?" she pouted.

Well, yeah. Someone patting you on the head in front of other people is gonna make you want to run screaming, all right?

"One more time."

For some reason—faced with the sight of her, hand in the air, face all scrunched up—I couldn't say no to her.

If my sister was still just a "girl" to me, I would've had no problem leaving her blowing in the wind. But now I had a different perspective on her. And that wasn't an option any longer.

I resigned myself to it, coming in closer. "Therrrre you go," she said as she ran a hand through my hair.

My body was frozen in place by the shame. I could see Kido grinning at the sight.

…How much longer will this go on?

I felt like I wanted this moment to end as soon as possible… and, simultaneously, continue on forever.

Looking back, maybe I transferred some of the emotion I used to reserve for my mother over to my sister on that day.

After all, from that moment—until the very, very end—I was incapable of defying my sister in any way at all.

ONE DAY, ON THE STREET

I plodded on in silence through the dimly lit street, making my way home.

I could feel no heat, nor any cold.

It was like all of my senses had gone haywire.

The image of the last time I saw my sister was burned into my mind in dull orange colors.

Where should I be heading toward? What should I do? I had no idea any longer.

At the very least, I had better do what that snake tells me to do.

If I don't, the two I left behind are gonna be in serious trouble.

The snake said it'd "kill" them. If I don't live up to my end of the bargain, that's gonna be a reality—in as cold and barbaric a way as possible.

I'm not allowed to choose when I die any longer.

Despite that, I couldn't talk to the rest of them.

The only force pushing my staggering legs forward was the words left in my mind by that snake.

"Huff...huff...Agh!"

As I kept walking, mind in a deep fog, I tripped and found myself hurtling to the ground, scraping a knee hard against the concrete. Pain ripped across my leg.

"...Ngh...!"

I grabbed on to a nearby light pole for support.

Oh, right: I needed to revert back to normal before returning home anyway. Maybe this was good timing, in a way.

If I stayed in the form of my sister for too long, that snake would...

*   *   *

...What am I even doing?
*My beloved sister is dead. Why do I have to pose as her corpse
and get all of those photos taken of me?* It was just pure torture.
Pure torture.
I wish it could just kill me already. *Why won't it?*

"Ugh...Damn it...!"

I was so pained, so helpless, I didn't know what to do.
What now? Somebody help me. Somebody...

"Ayano...? Ooh, I thought it was you, Ayano."
I turned toward the voice. Under the dim streetlight, I saw
the form of Shintaro Kisaragi.
"What're you doing down there?"
Wait. I just felt all that pain. Why wasn't I back to my normal
form?
...Oh, crap. This is awful. And I just *had* to run into him...

"What? You feeling okay? ...Oh, I bet the summer-school
teacher yelled at you about something, didn't he? Eesh. You
know that happens to you because you never study, right? I just
gave you that tutoring session and everything, too..."
"...Shut up."
"Wh-what...? Geez, you don't have to stare daggers at me
like that..."

I pushed Shintaro Kisaragi aside and walked away.
"Hey! Hey, what's up with you, man? You're acting weird!"
I turned around one final time and addressed him directly:

"This is all *your* fault. You never noticed *any* of it."

The night was drawing near.

Outside the window, the sun was slowly being swallowed up by the rectangular outlines of the buildings below. In the blink of an eye, it fell below them and disappeared, leaving only a dim afterglow behind.

The homes, bathed in an orange glare, slowly began to be enveloped in blackness. Nobody could stop night from coming now.

It was true. That was the way the world worked. It wasn't going to show me any mercy from the start.

I couldn't turn back time, and I certainly couldn't make it go any faster. *No matter who lives or who dies, the world goes at the same speed it always does.*

These incredibly obvious laws of nature seemed all the more vibrant to me as I groggily stared out the window.

Lying on my back in bed, I turned my eyes away from the window and turned my body to the side to follow them. The bookshelf that entered my sight featured a neatly arranged selection of superhero comics that I hadn't touched in a while.

How long ago was it when I used to pretend I was a hero, fantasizing about all the exciting adventures I'd join the ones on TV in? Or when we used to run around the neighborhood, pretending that we were a group of undercover superheroes ourselves?

The more I thought back on it, the more I reflected on how much had happened over the past few years.

We tried to go to school but never quite fit in—and when it finally all fell apart, the three of us cried the whole night through in frustration.

All the notebooks, textbooks, school uniforms my mother and father bought us...It all went to waste. I felt terrible about that.

They told me to do my best, but I couldn't keep my part of the bargain. That was the most painful thing of all.

I think it was around then that Seto tried to skip out of town, no longer able to stand the grief his powers gave him.

I thought he was just going out to let off some steam, but he still wasn't back after dark, which made me fear the worst for some time.

The entire family went out to search for him, of course—but, really, that wasn't as hard as trying to console my sister, sobbing loudly throughout the hunt.

When Seto returned the next day, the first words out of his mouth were "I met this cute girl." My reaction went beyond anger and into the realm of exasperation.

Kido beat the stuffing out of him, as everyone expected. Strangely, though, Seto managed to keep his powers a lot more under control after that point.

Maybe it was thanks to that "cute girl" he supposedly met in some forest somewhere. They were still getting along well, I heard, but given how reluctant he was to let us see her, I was starting to have my suspicions.

Kido, for her part, had softened considerably from before. Her own power wasn't causing as much trouble for her any longer, either.

She "got the knack" of it is how she boastfully described it. But being able to flick her presence on and off at will created other problems.

Back when Seto and I were joking about her to ourselves, she appeared right by our side and said, "What's *that* supposed to mean?" I thought I was gonna go into cardiac arrest.

And on that topic, the conflict over excessive apologies that raged for years between Kido and Seto was finally in its closing stages.

Apparently, Kido's hang-up over it stemmed from the habits of the people she used to live with, way back when. "I didn't want any more friends who did that," she explained.

Since she opened up with that, Seto made a serious effort to improve—though if anything, it made his speech even more awkward than it should have been. I had just about gotten used to it as of late, although it was kind of sad to see the old Seto become a thing of the past.

Still, they were getting along much better than before, so I couldn't complain.

The two of them made an effort to change, and they did.

The only one who didn't—who never even tried—might be me, lying here in the middle of the room.

This had happened before, once, me spending the whole day doing nothing, sitting in my room and thinking about assorted things.

About when my mother—the one who gave birth to me, that is—died.

I really thought, back then, that life would just go on for me. Like I was floating in space, nothing reaching out. Happiness wasn't something I even dared to hope for.

But how did that work out?

I was blessed with new parents, new siblings, and a life that I could spend smiling and laughing all day.

It seemed like some kind of fever dream, sometimes. Like the world had seen what I went through and finally said, "Let there be happiness."

Until a month ago—until Ayaka, the mother who brought me to this point, passed away—I seriously believed in all that crap.

"...Why did it have to wind up like this?"
I whined to myself, a habit I easily fell into. I suppose if the world had ears attached to it, I could point my grief in that direction. But it didn't. And if it did, I'd probably try to tear them off instead.
If the world gained conscious thought overnight, I'd gouge it out from the core, smash it against the ground, and stomp it flat.
The more I thought about it, the more it made my stomach churn, like my guts were going to spew out of my mouth.
What did *we* ever do to anyone?
We accepted life in this world, held back our tears against injustice, gritted our teeth against unfairness, and thought we finally obtained happiness. And now look.
How did we let it get taken from us so, so easily?
Did the world dislike us so much that it wouldn't even allow a tiny sliver of happiness for us?
Who was it? Who created this putrid world, anyway...?

"What're *you* moping about?"
I sat up, startled by the sudden voice, only to find Kido staring down at me in a hoodie and a pair of sweatpants.
Her hair used to be short and frizzy. Now it came down to her shoulders, making her look much more female even as her face remained cold and indifferent to the world.
"Y-you were here?"

There was no telling how long she might've been observing me. She was that skillful with it now.

"What? Something got you down?"

Kido remained expressionless, but it seemed like she was worried for me. Hurriedly, I stuck a "smile" on my face.

"N-no, no! I'm not moping about anything, man! Like, I'm feeling *super*-great right now. Uh, maybe you're worried 'cause I was sleeping by myself? Geez, Kido, that's awful cute of you... Ow!"

My simpering nonsense was cut short by a sudden conk on the head.

"Wh-what'd you go and do *that* for?!"

I held my head as I pleaded my case. Kido paused a bit before answering.

"...You're crying, you big liar."

I didn't notice until then.

The "smile" I pasted on my face was gone. My deceiving powers were temporarily dissolved by the pain.

"Oof..."

The real expression I had under the smile...I couldn't say how she gauged that one. I hid my face, not expecting its tear-soaked visage to be exposed to the world like this.

"N-no! Seriously, I'm not crying! Man, you're such a bully..."

I can't believe a little bop on the head was enough to cancel my power. *This thing's useless, isn't it?*

I tried my hardest to freshen up my reddened face, but it was a little too late for that now. Not to mention meaningless.

With a heavy sigh, Kido crouched down and whispered, "Idiot" into my ear.

"I-idiot...?"

I wasn't able to chain any more words together.

"You don't have to pretend," Kido continued. "It's not healthy to do that."

She certainly had a point. I was pretty much screaming "Please! Worry about me!" to her with my act. I saw no way out.

"...I'm sorry. My bad."

This past month had to have taken its toll on Kido, too. I saw her crying on multiple occasions myself. She really didn't have the emotional capacity to worry about me, too, but here I was making her do it anyway. *I am such an idiot.*

"It's all right. You're such an idiot, you can't help it."

The venom-laden forgiveness put my mind at ease a little.

"I'll keep on punching you, though. For *your* sake, okay?"

Now my mind *wasn't* so at ease. *I suppose I'm destined for a short life.*

"Ah-ha-ha...What're you in here for, though? Did you need something?"

"Oh, right. Big Sis said it's time to eat. Dad and Seto are waiting for you."

Kido pointed a finger at the door. I stood up in a rush.

"Huh? Everybody's home already?! Agh, I'm sorry! I'll be right out!"

"You waste *so* much of my time," she gruffly replied as she left.

I couldn't agree with her more. Even *I* thought so. But although she was a little rough around the edges, Kido was always kind to me when it counted.

Ahh, look at the mistake I've been making. I've still been happy this whole time, haven't I?

It's not like back when I was all alone. I've got someone kind enough to punch me now.

I have to keep on living. I need to get happy.

If I'm not happy, I start dragging down the rest of the family with me.

…Yeah. I won't let the world just have its way with me like this. No way. I need to survive, survive, and get happy, no matter what.

"Wonder what we're having…? Hopefully nothing like the horrors we've had lately."

"I think we're safe there. Smells kinda weird, but…"

"Aw, man, seriously? …Ah, well. Better learn how to cook before I bitch about it. Kinda wish you'd cook sometime, though, Kido. You're a lot better at it."

"Sure. I don't mind. But you know how much Big Sis insists on doing it all the time. Can't do much about that."

We headed for the dining table as we spoke.

Dinner tasted about as iffy as I expected, but—for a nice change of pace—I was able to laugh with my family a little tonight.

*

A typical day in spring.

I was milling around a small park near my house. I was there because my sister told me to report over there. That she had something she wanted to ask about.

Looking over the sparse selection of playground equipment, I opted to sit down on a swing. There wasn't much to do, so I indifferently stared at the sky.

By this point, I was used to my sister saying weird stuff to me without warning. If anything, I was thankful for the fact she gave me plenty of advance notice this time. Not long ago, she tore into our room, said, "Let's go out and do something

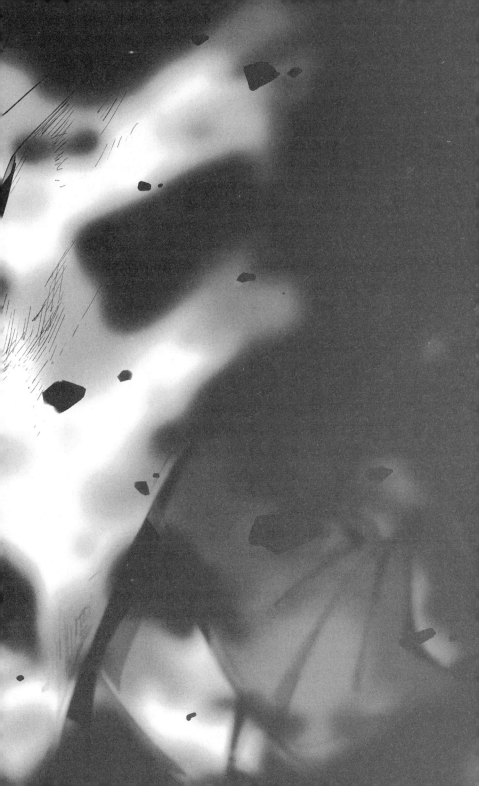

fun!" and then she dragged us out to go catch insects until the middle of the night.

Compared to that, a little chat in the park was child's play. Assuming it really *was* nothing more than a chat. I had my doubts, considering she was luring me out to the park for this. Something a little awkward to bring up at home, maybe?

Now that I thought about it, my sister had been acting a bit depressed lately.

Usually, she was *super*-upbeat all the time. The "super" adjective was needed in order to fully encompass how much energy she had. Contrast that with how she was acting now, and it seemed fair to assume that the topic she wanted to discuss had something to do with her recent funk.

She was in high school now, for one, and she mentioned that the classes were getting a lot harder for her. *Maybe it's that... but then again, why'd she want to talk to me about that? That's more of a Dad topic.*

So some kind of nonschool issue, then. For example...

"...Love, or something?"

Saying it out loud to myself instantly filled me with shame.

No way. Not my *sister*, of all people. She was a walking encyclopedia of boys' comics and superhero TV series. She didn't have time for any of that *romance*-type stuff. It was crazy to even consider the thought. Totally crazy...

"Yeah. Crazy!"

I jumped off the swings, the chains clanging in agreement with me.

This was my sister's business, of course. She had every right to do what she wanted with her own life. I knew that.

But what if she's really fallen in love with somebody?

What if it's just some random chump off the street? What then?

...It'd be a bloodbath.

The entire family would probably strip the poor guy's bones clean in a second. Once Dad found out, in particular, it'd be hell on earth for the dude. He'd wipe the guy completely out of existence, as if he'd never been born. And I'd help, of course.

But. One big but. If that actually happened to my sister, *and* she wanted to talk about it with somebody, who would she turn to? Seto would be too embarrassed to help out at all, and Kido would provide even less of a useful contribution. Assuming Dad was out of the question, there was only one family member left.

"Me...? Ugh...Pressure's on."

It was all guesswork on my part, but it seemed ominously plausible.

The way I heard it, once you're high-school age, it's perfectly normal to have at least one or two boyfriends.

...Wait, "one or two"? *Over my dead body, she will!*

But there was nothing I could do to deny the possibility. It wouldn't be strange at all to have her bound up to me and say, "Ooh, I think I *found* someone!"

And she *did* mention that she "made a really good friend" earlier. They went to last year's school festival together, she reported, and they played some kind of wacky target-shooting game. They were even in the same homeroom together.

So, connect the dots, and...

"...Him?"

It was all guesses and imaginings, but my eyes were honed like a hunter's gun sight against my virtual enemy. *I dare him to lay a hand on my sister. Because if he ever does...*

"Heyyyy, sorry I'm late!"

My sister bellowed her presence as she ran into the park, wearing her usual winter school uniform topped with a scarf around her neck. I'm not sure when the transition took place, but she couldn't have looked more like a teenage girl in her prime if she tried. I tucked my theories into a drawer in my mind.

"Hey, Sis, what's up? You didn't have to be in that big of a hurry."

"Oh, no, I didn't want to keep you waiting, so…"

She giggled, a little shyly. That innocence of hers was unchanged from the past, but once she reached high school, she started maturing at breathtaking speed. Maybe I was a little biased, but I didn't think there were many girls out there as nice as she was.

"But, hey, sorry to make you come out here outta nowhere!"

"Oh, it's fine. Not like you've ever given me a lot of notice before now. So, what's up?"

"Well, um…"

Ayano seemed to have trouble getting started. I silently waited for her to continue, but she doggedly refused to open her mouth until I caved.

"What is it?"

"No, I mean, it's kind of hard to say, you know? Like, I don't know where to begin."

She tried her best to cover her emotions. But I could tell she was reluctant to even be here with me. The presumptions I made in my mind earlier began bubbling back to the surface.

"Well…What? Is it that serious, or…?"

Was it really about a guy after all? Just when it began to seriously disturb me, my sister, finally summoning up enough resolve, parted her lips.

"…No, uh…You know. It's about why Mom died."

"Bwuhh?"

I failed to provide a coherent reply. *This* was a totally different direction than what I was prepared for.

Ayano turned her eyes downward.

"I mean, they said Mom died in landslide, right?"

Ayaka—my new mother—worked as an archaeologist, mostly conducting her research in the field of folklore.

Thanks to the demands of this unusual career, she was never at home all that much, usually flying off to this or that field site.

On that fateful day, too, she was out on location with my father. Or so they told us.

"Yeah. I heard about that, too. They were doing some kind of field research, right?"

"Yeah. And I know that's true, but…Hey, you wanna sit down somewhere? These shoes are still pinching me a little."

Ayano tapped the edge of one of her loafers against the ground. I followed her to a nearby bench.

"But I got this…"

Once we were both seated, she took a notebook out of her schoolbag. It wasn't old, but heavy use had left it tattered around the edges. The front cover was neatly labeled with the title MONSTER INVESTIGATION RECORDS.

"'Monster'? What's that about? …Is this Mom's? Where'd you find something like…?"

I reached out to take it. My sister kept it away from me.

"Whoa! What're you…What, I'm not allowed to read it?"

"W-wait a minute! I'm sorry, but…"

She held the notebook against her body. Taking a more careful look, I noticed she was shaking, tears just beginning to form at the corners of her eyes. This was absolutely *not* normal behavior for her.

"Look, what's wrong with you?! Are you feeling okay…?"

"Nnh, sorry," she weakly bubbled as I rubbed her back. "It's not that. It's just…I'm kinda scared."

All these unnerving things she was saying began to throw my mind into chaos. What kind of horrifying things could be written in there, anyway? If it was about a "monster," it had to be something pretty freaky.

My sister took two or three deep breaths to compose herself.

"I'm sorry. I'm probably freaking you out right now. I wanted you to read this, Shuuya, but…before you do, can we talk a little bit?"

She stared right into my eyes as she asked. From them I could feel an intensity, a sense of resolve, that was never there usually.

"Well, sure. Anything you want, just let me know."

"Thanks," she said, her face a little saddened. "Shuuya, do you remember when we used to pretend we were a bunch of superheroes with secret identities?"

"Sure. We'd put on hoodies and pretend to fly around and stuff. We called ourselves…"

"… The Mekakushi-dan."

Ayano came up with it before I did. The name brought back memories. Whenever we were together, that's what we did—team up, form the Mekakushi-dan in our imaginations, and save the town from evil.

"These 'eye powers'.…That was a secret shared just between the four of us. We had to hide them away from the world…so we were the Mekakushi-dan."

She paused, rolling her eyes a little.

"…Kind of a silly name, looking back on it, huh?"

Probably, yeah. I could come up with something a lot cooler sounding now.

Still, I liked that name. Hindsight is 20/20, of course, but in a way, that was my sister taking our eyes—these things that people feared, treating them as taboos to be shunned—and hiding them from the public for me. That was what the group was for. She declared herself the leader, got us all hoodies to make it easier to hide our "eyes," and kept us smiling the whole time through. That was our sister.

But why's she bringing that up now? I still had trouble sensing where this conversation was going.

"Why're you talking about that again? Does that have something to do with what you wanted to ask me?"

"…Yeah."

Ayano took another deep breath, then slowly began to speak again.

"Mom, you know…I think she knew about all of those 'eye powers' from the very start. She knew how much grief they caused everyone, too."

"What?! No way! I *know* I hid mine, at least! I had to do whatever it took to keep from getting kicked out of here…!"

"I know. I know, Shuuya. But I had no idea…No idea that Mom was trying to save you all…from those 'snake powers'…"

My sister began crying. Small droplets formed on the dry ground. She didn't try to wipe them off, clutching the notebook tightly against her chest as she let out a sob.

"This is getting really bad…I don't know what to do…but I think it might kill all of us…!"

I was powerless.

Unable to do anything for my sister as she broke down into uncontrollable sobbing.

Unable even to understand the reality that was suddenly thrust before me.

In fact, I really knew nothing.

Nothing about the sad creatures this notebook called

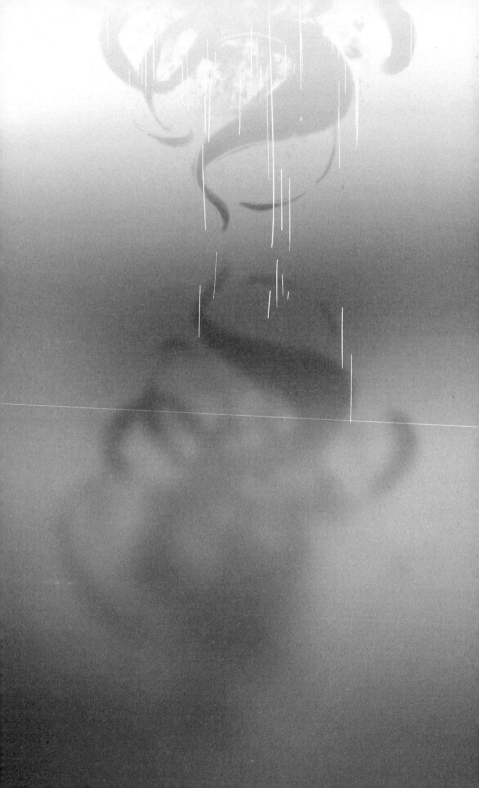

"monsters." Nothing about the "curse" we carried within us. And nothing about my father, either...

What little shred of "happiness" we had remaining by that point was already rotted to pieces, beyond all repair.

*

"...So I think the 'Snake of Clearing Eyes' that possessed Dad is trying to make his wish come true for him."

"His wish...?"

"Yeah. He wants to see Mom again, one more time."

"Can...can he do that?"

"Supposedly, he can, if he can create a monster in *this* world. That way, he can meet up with people swallowed into the *other* world..."

"...Well, great, then! Can we help him out at—?"

"No!!"

"Huh...?"

"...If you want to create a monster, you have to gather up a bunch of snakes to substitute for your own life. You have to form them all into one...so..."

"You mean...our...?"

"I want to see Mom again, too...but if everyone has to die to make that happen, then...No. Just no...!"

"Sis..."

"Mom worried so much about us, right up to the end. We can't let anything like this happen...Never...!"

*

"The older students you know...Those guys?"

"Yeah. You met 'em at school, right, Shuuya? Takane and

Haruka…That snake's trying to possess both of them with the remaining snakes on the other side. I think it's gonna try to swallow them into the other world."

"You mean it's gonna kill 'em?! …But he can't go that far! The police aren't just gonna let that happen!"

"I looked into it myself! While you were going to school for me, Shuuya! That snake's already done all kinds of horrible things in Dad's body…He's got a ton of money. He's got hospitals, he's got schools, he's got the police…And other bad guys way high up, too. They're all helping that snake out…"

"N-no way…"

"So listen, Shuuya. I'm thinking about trying to make contact with that snake. I think that's the only option we've got left…"

"Huh?! We can't! This guy who kills people on a whim like that?! What makes you think it'll bother listening to us…?!"

"You don't think so? Well, I'm so stupid, maybe that'll throw it off enough to start talking, y'know?"

"Don't be so dumb, Sis! If I have to lose you, too, I'd…"

"Oh, what're you talking about? I'm not planning on going anywhere. I'm staying right here. With all you guys. So don't cry, all right?"

"No…You can't do that…I can't live in a world without you, Sis…!"

"It'll be fine, okay? Look, you didn't forget, did you, Shuuya? I'm the leader of the Mekakushi-dan! I could whip one or two of those guys, no sweat! So listen…Don't start hating the world on me again, okay?

" 'Cause it's gonna be a happy one for all of us pretty soon."

*

"Sis! No!!"

*   *   *

I flung the door open and flew outside.

My sister's hair whirled in the howling night gusts as she stood at the edge of the roof.

Her body, completely bathed in orange, seemed fleeting to me, ready to be sucked into the sky at any moment.

"Shuuya...!"

She called my name, terror clear upon her face.

"Don't do anything like that! You said we'd be together... That you'd always be there for me!"

The words made Ayano grimace in anguish. But she didn't waver.

"...If we know the plan's not going to work, there's no point going on with it! This way, those two students don't have to die for good. Or our family."

Then she turned toward the wide-open night sky. Another step, and there would be no more resistance between her body and the ground.

"Stop! Sis, stop!!"

I screamed as loud as I could. But my sister neither pulled back nor turned to see me again.

"This way, I'm taking the dead in with me."

As she spoke, a dark sort of haze shimmered around her for just a moment. I had seen that before. The saddest existence there was in this world.

I thought I was going to go insane.

From the bottom of my heart, I prayed that the next instant

would never arrive. I pleaded to this world, the one I hated so much, to just stop everything.

I don't care who it is. Just help me. Save me...and save my sister.

She spoke through the sobs.

"I'm sorry, Shuuya. It's not very cool of me as a big sister, I guess, but...I'm kind of scared."

Even if I ran at full speed, I wouldn't be in time.

Powerless, I felt something snap and tear itself apart in my mind as my sister left her body to the wind, disappearing from sight.

"Ugh...I never thought it'd wind up like this. I'm so exasperated with these guys, I don't know what to say."

"...I'm gonna kill you."

"Whoa, whoa, get ahold of yourself. You know full well I'm the one who let your father live, don't you? There's no need to go around making threats like that...Although she certainly did a great job ruining our plans. Now that we can't gather up all the snakes, we can't bring him his wife back. How wonderful..."

"Just do nothing, then. Just...give me my father back, at least...!"

"What are you, stupid? If we failed once, we'll just try it again. From the top...Hey, I know. Why don't you pretend to be her corpse for us? You're good at that sort of thing, right? That way,

once they find you, the other guys I have control over will just chalk it up to suicide. Having her disappear without a trace, you know…That would present a lot of lingering problems."

"What the hell are you—?!"

"Hey, don't get the wrong idea. I'm the one allowing both you and your family to stay alive. Or would you prefer to see them dismembered before your eyes? Probably not, am I right?"

"Ngh…hhh…"

"Your power's pretty useful to me, all right? Just do what I tell you to do, and I'll make sure nothing bad happens, got it? …*Got* it? You know nothing's gonna change your destiny. No matter what you try. So unless you want an early grave for you and your family, you better watch your step."

"Damn it…Damn it…!"

"All you bastards are being kept alive on the palm of my hand. Don't forget that, you little brat."

TODAY, ON THE STREET

I wonder if that girl made it back to her body.

Not that it'd make much difference, I don't think. At least I got to say what I wanted to say, in the end.

After all that yapping I had to endure, during all those lunch sessions on the roof, I felt I had the right to complain at least a little to finish the process off.

Yet, I couldn't say how long it's been since I talked to another person.

For all I know, it could be the very first time.

The fact that I've been able to go on and on about my personal story like this...It's all thanks to that girl with the twisted personality, I suppose.

It was weird, but there were bits and pieces of us that scarily resembled each other. Not that it matters much, any longer.

The streetlights lit the nighttime path I walked at regular intervals, their dim glow filling me with an odd sense of reassurance.

With every step, the tapping of my feet resonated pleasantly in my ears. I can't say exactly since when, but I was starting to like nights like these.

A pure shade of black concealed the pallid color of my own strained face.

A rabble of needless, putrid utterances covered up the night wind for me.

The darkness was willing to forgive even this warped, hideous heart.

*   *   *

...Have I changed somewhere along the line?
I couldn't even tell any longer. It exasperated me.
Not even the pain was enough to remind me of who I was.
By now, I was completely unable to ascertain where the "me" was in me.

But, I figured, there wasn't any need to think about it any longer.

In just a little longer, everything will be over.
A blackness, incomparably darker even than the darkness I dwelt in, was going to crush me and all of my other powerless acquaintances.

...Still, I wasn't very nice to those kids yesterday.
I wished I could have let that group go, at the very least. But it was out of my hands.
It said that the "snakes" instinctively sought to gather toward their "queen," and I suppose those kids were no exception.

I couldn't change a single thing.
As much as I struggled to in places, everything fell into place exactly as It said it would. Uncanny.
And if this world really was created for the reasons It gave me, I had no chance from the beginning.

What really *is* happiness, in the end?
At this point, I was starting to feel like we never had it from the get-go.
Even those days I spent at that house started to seem like the product of an overactive imagination to me.

*   *   *

Suddenly, I stopped, hearing the sound of someone else's footsteps.

Looking in the direction of the sound, I saw the familiar sight of Seto.

"Ahhh! I finally found you!"

Seto gave me an exaggerated wave, then made a beeline toward me.

"Eesh, I've been looking for you ever since I got off work! You're so mean! If you're gonna go somewhere, you really oughta tell me!"

"Wh-what'd you go and do *that* for? It's no big deal. I'm just out for a bit."

Seto frowned at me.

"Wha?! Everyone was worried sick about you yesterday, too! If you can't get back, you could at least call or something!"

Something about his lecturing tone began to irk me. *Where does he get off, acting all high and mighty? He doesn't know a thing.*

"All right, all right," I spat out. "Stop griping at me."

"Oh, quit putting it that way," Seto whined. "I'm worried about you, too, you know."

...I could understand what he was saying well enough.

I knew full well they're really worried about me, too.

But, as much as I hated to admit it, as much as I had lost hold of myself, "my" heart was in pieces, painfully ripped apart. The inky cloud of emotion that poured out of it made it impossible for me to do anything any longer.

"Shut up!! Geez, just lay the hell off me already!"

My shout echoed across the street.

"Quit going on and on like you know everything about me! 'Cause you don't, all right?! Acting like you're some kind of golden boy! You act like you care about me on the outside, but…"

My emotions thrust themselves out in all directions. I lost track of everything I was saying.

"Wh-what's all that coming from…?"

"It…It's from the way you're *talking* to me!! What the hell…? Why…?"

I fell to the ground on my knees, tears rolling out of my eyes.

"Why'd you all have to change…? You, Seto, and Kido, too… Why hasn't anyone noticed *me*?! Sis went and died all by herself…It's too much…"

It felt like everything within me was collapsing into a giant heap of garbage.

"I can't take it…this *world*, anymore…"

"Kano…"

Seto, crouching down, pulled my shoulder toward him.

"It's all right…It's all right…"

"What is…? *What's* all right, for God's sake…?"

Nothing was all right.

I wished this whole world would just end for me. Then, I could…

"I'm sorry I never noticed for you…I know I was near you this whole time, too…"

All I could do now was trust in Seto's words.

"…I can't do it. I'm so scared, I couldn't talk to anyone…so…"

Seto patted me on the back. I felt like I was going to fall apart at any moment.

"I know. I'm sorry I made you carry it all by yourself…Let's carry it together."

* * *

"I mean, we're brothers."

That had a nostalgic ring to it.
I recalled the night we spent in secret conversation at Room 107 of the special-care facility.

I seem to remember laughing things off. Saying "Well, great" a lot more often.

*

Seto and I walked back to the hideout.

I wondered what was up with everyone. I never told them about any of this before. Maybe they'd hate me afterward.

"Oh, they won't. You'll be fine."

Seto's statement made me shiver with fright.

"Y-you used your power again…? That's sure been a while. Kind of embarrassing, getting read like that."

"Huhh?! Didn't you just say you wanted us to listen to you?"

"Dahh! That's in the past, all right? …Seriously, though, don't tell everybody else about that, all right?"

"Ha-ha-ha! No problem! It'll be a secret between men!"

Seto grinned at me. I kept my head down. This night was proving to be a major embarrassment to me.

"Ugh, this is *so* out of character for me. Agghh…"

"Well, what's the harm with that sometimes?"

Seto was acting just as bright and jovial as always. I wasn't sure he truly understood the weight of the situation.

Even if he did, though, he'd probably still act like this.

He used to be such a pathetic crybaby. Now he was one of the most relied-upon presences in my life.

As we chatted on the way home, I noticed someone standing in front of a set of vending machines.

"Oh, great…I *really* don't wanna run into her…"

The figure, noticing me, began to walk on up. She had on some kind of hospital gown that she probably swiped from somewhere, her long black hair done up in a pair of ponytails.

"Hmm? Who's that?"

"…Ene."

My identification broke Seto's brain for a few moments.

Which I could understand. We were talking the difference between two and three dimensions here, after all. Not too many people are going to swallow that on the first try.

"Huhhh?! I thought Ene was more…like, smaller than that."

"*Who's* smaller, huh? Who?"

The sharp-eyed girl approaching us glared at Seto.

"Eee?! Uh, no…"

His eyes rolled up in terror. I stepped up to take the slack.

"Would it be better to call you Takane, then?"

Takane looked even less appreciative of that.

"I…I don't care. It's all a big pain in the ass, anyway."

"Umm…All right. Well, I gotta call you something, so Takane it is, then."

"Whatever…," she gruffly replied.

"But…Wow, you're looking a lot better, aren't you? You looked like you were gonna die a little bit ago."

"Yeahhh, well, I've had a few ups and downs. Also, if you won't mind, I'd like you to keep our last little chat secret from the rest of the gang, if you could…"

Takane gave me a devilish grin. She always was twisted like that. Just like me.

"Oh, come on! You're that embarrassed about disguising yourself as your sister and going to school for her? Hmm…*Innn*-teresting."

Great. I knew it was a mistake to talk to her. It was like adding oil to the fire.

"Well, I'm impressed you decided to come back, Takane. You looked like you were having a blast as Ene."

The moment I mentioned the name, Takane crouched to the ground, head in her hands.

"Ooh, I wanna die, I wanna die, I wanna die, I wanna die…"

Guess I had a few weapons of my own.

"Oh, maaan, I have no idea what I'm gonna do. He's gonna, like, totally freak."

I imagine he will, yes. Hanging out around her sworn enemy, calling him "master," running roughshod over him all the way to today...

...I guess I better apologize to Shintaro, too.

I know I had been angry, but there was no taking back what I did. It was pretty mean, actually. I doubted he'd forgive me, but I at least wanted to give him the whole story...

"What? You worried about him or something?"

Takane must have noticed. She looked up, still in her anguished crouch.

"Well...yeah. I kind of owe him one, you know?"

"Hmm...Well, he's not stupid. I don't think he'll hold it against you that much, once you clue him in a little. There's a lot of stuff I gotta discuss with him, too, so...How about we all talk together?"

"...Yeah. Sounds good."

Takane, I suppose, had a unique insight into what made Shintaro tick. Lord knew they'd spent enough time together.

Then she started grabbing her head again.

"But oh, *man*, I don't know...Just thinking about him makes me wanna barf..."

"What? Aw, come on, Takane! Plus, you haven't eaten for, like, two years! You don't have anything to barf out!"

"I just had some ramen."

"What'd you pay for it with?!"

"Geez, lay off me! I was hungry, all right?! Two years, man, *two years*!! That'd give anyone a hankering for a steaming bowl of pork *chashu-men*!"

"Yeah, and how'd you *pay* for it...?"

*   *   *

Seto, watching silently, raised a hand into the air.

I guess we kind of left him by the side of the road in this conversation.

"Um, I don't think I really get what you're talking about..."

His eyes were darting between us in utter confusion.

I was happy to explain things, but we were about to hold a crash course for the whole gang back at our hideout. I opted to wait until then.

Nice of him not to try reading my mind, at least. *That's Seto for you.*

"...Well, we're gonna have to go through a lot of crap pretty soon, so I figure we'll explain everything to everyone all at once. Save us some time that way. So how 'bout we just head back?"

Takane and Seto muttered "yeah" in simultaneous agreement.

"So if you're back," I asked Takane, "I guess you're ready to do this, huh?"

She snorted back at me.

"Of course! I promised that to Ayano, besides. I just have to punch out that bearded freak, right? I'm not gonna call this over until I do, so..."

Takane, eyes sparkling, apparently didn't know what I meant. But, considering the circumstances, I was glad she was rarin' to go.

Seto slapped me on the back.

"I'll try to talk with Marie about this, too. I dunno...This might get kind of hairy on us, but if we all work together, I think we'll find a way!"

"Oww...Yeah. Seems kind of stupid, huh? Trying to carry it all by yourself."

I couldn't help but laugh at the sound of *me* saying that.

Even when faced with the end of the world, nothing changes between us.

I thought everyone except me had changed. I was barking up the wrong tree the whole time.

Takane looked at me, bewildered.

"Wow. So that's how you smile, huh?"

"Huh?"

"It sure is! Kano gets flustered pretty easily, so he almost never smiles!"

My face began to redden in front of my companions. Takane immediately flew in for the kill.

"Oooo! Trying to hide something again?"

"Sh-shut up! C'mon, let's get back already!"

"Sure thing! Man, I'm hungry, though. Better get something to eat back home!"

"I, uh, I just had ramen, so..."

...Sis.
You watching us?

Things have gotten a lot more hectic than before, but I guess we haven't changed much after all.

We're gonna be back playing our little superhero game in a sec, too. Funny, huh?

*　　*　　*

...Hey, Sis?

I'm gonna be with him soon. That guy you liked. And I'm gonna tell him everything.

He's kind of a wimp, and honestly I don't like him too much, but something about him...He's interesting, you know?

Something tells me he's just the guy to get Dad back, to get the world back, and to get you back, too. Pretty crazy story, I know, but...

Oh, right. Don't worry about losing your number. As far as we're concerned, No. 0's been retired from the Mekakushi-dan. So once you're back, let's all join in the game together, okay?

I hope you don't mind...

...waiting just a bit longer for us, Sis.

AFTERWORD

Pulling the Wool Away from Your Eyes

Hi. JIN here. How did you like *Kagerou Daze, Vol. 5: The Deceiving*?

The hero of this volume was, as you know, the young man Kano. Compared to the narrative characters from previous volumes, he's definitely a bit crankier, a bit harder to grasp, and certainly a lot more difficult to write from his perspective. That's what makes him so adorable, though. Hopefully, he, Shintaro, and the rest of the gang can become friends in a real way going forward.

A lot of people seem to like Kano the character, which I appreciate immensely. As I mentioned in the previous afterword, my cousin is one of Kano's many fans. *Totally* popular with the ladies, in other words. I couldn't be more jealous.

Thus, I figured I'd use this volume to have Kano throw up once or twice, but due to structuring difficulties, I had to edit it all out. Lucky for him, I suppose.

By the way, my mother apparently likes Shintaro. I suppose that doesn't matter much, but hey.

The Deceiving is the subtitle this time around, and it was actually a pretty arduous process getting to that.

I think we went through a few iterations along those lines, like *The Deceiver* and *The Night of Deception* and so on. It wound up being a two-horse race between *My Wacky Sister-Swapping Cross-Dressing School Fantasy* and *The Deceiving*, and for some reason I couldn't convince anyone else to vote for the first one, so here we are. It's always hard to decide on these things.

So we're now at Volume 5 of the novels. Slowly but surely, we're getting closer to the end.

The closer we get, the sadder it makes me feel, in a way. This is my first shot at being a published novelist, and I'm wondering to myself whether there's still a bit more life to this story after all. I'll devote everything I have to writing this up to the end, and while it may not be for much longer, I hope you'll be watching and reading to see how the characters develop.

Though, really, I never would've come this far without the warm support I've received from all of you.

I tend to do a lot of research (time-wasting) on the Net while writing, and whenever I look at all the fan fiction and illustrations people have drawn of Mekakushi-dan members, it really just makes me incredibly happy.

Some of you are drawing Mekakushi-dan manga as well, which I'm also digging a great deal. Thanks much.

Come to think of it, there hasn't been a volume of this series covering the characters' normal daily lives yet. In fact, we have yet to see all ten members in the same place. That's something I'd like to cover in novel form sometime. It'd be nice if I had the chance, anyway.

Anyway, this volume was another test of my skills as I tried to write about this cast's adventures without letting their personalities overwhelm me.

What was that? The publishing schedule's slowing down from before? Oh, no, no, it's not because I'm getting lazy. In fact, I'm mind-bendingly busy as always. In parallel with this novel, I'm participating in live shows, producing the intro songs for video games, writing anime scripts, producing the intro song for said anime, etc., etc...

......

Hey, we're an anime now!! (Did I forget to mention that?)

Yes, it's true. *Mekakucity Actors*, an anime series that depicts the *Kagerou* characters in a brand-new story, is going to be broadcast nationwide! (Is that ad copy hot enough for you?)

I'm really, really excited about this. It makes me realize all the more that, if you put your creative mind to it, you really can make your dreams come true. That, as well, is all thanks to your kind support. Seriously.

I think we'll be able to get Volume 6 released before too long. It'd be great if you could keep on supporting this effort.

See you in the next afterword!

JIN (Shizen no Teki-P)

Beauty mark

SIDU

Volume 5
Novel
Released!
Congratulations!!

The Mekakucity Actors anime is just about to kick off!! Kano acted even more troll-like than ever before! I love it!! Lately, it's really hit home to me that this truly is a series a lot of people love. I can hardly wait to see what happens next!!

On the manga side of things, we're currently producing an original story penned by JIN exclusively for the manga! Thanks a lot for all your hard work, JIN...!! The story over here's pretty exciting, too! I hope you'll enjoy all the differences between the novels, anime, and manga!

kano

MAHIRO SATOU

VOLUME 5 ON SALE! CONGRATS!!

THANKS FOR THE HARD WORK, JIN AND SIDU! EVERY TIME I WRITE ONE OF THESE CONGRATULATORY LETTERS, I ALWAYS THINK TO MYSELF, "MAN, IT'D BE NICE IF I COULD CATCH UP TO THEM..." BUT! THIS YEAR, I PROMISE I'LL WORK TO NOT JUST CATCH UP, BUT SURPASS YOU GUYS! SO YOU BETTER WATCH OUT! AND WATCH YOUR DIET, TOO! THERE'S MORE TO LIFE THAN BURGERS, YOU KNOW!

THIS IS RYUUSEI!!

YOUR EVER-HUMBLE ILLUSTRATOR

TWITTER
↳ @RYUUSEEE

KAGEROU

Congratulations on Releasing Volume 5!

Whenever I saw JIN scrambling in a mad dash to meet his deadlines, I thought to myself, "Man, I hope he doesn't work himself to death..." But it looks like everything worked out okay with this volume, huh? Congrats!

I'll be doing my best going forward, too... and, of course, I'll be looking forward to what JIN comes up with next!

Hey, it's Kano.

Ishiburo

Cover Illustration Sketch

* Illustration split in half. This is the left side.

* Right side

Frontispiece Sketch

Illustration 1 Sketch

Illustration 2 Sketch

Illustration 3 Sketch

Illustration 4 Sketch

Illustration 5 Sketch

Illustration 6 Sketch

* Printed vertically for space reasons

Illustration 7 Sketch

Azami?
Snake?
Kagerou Daze?

The blurred cloud...

* Printed vertically for space reasons

Illustration 8 Sketch

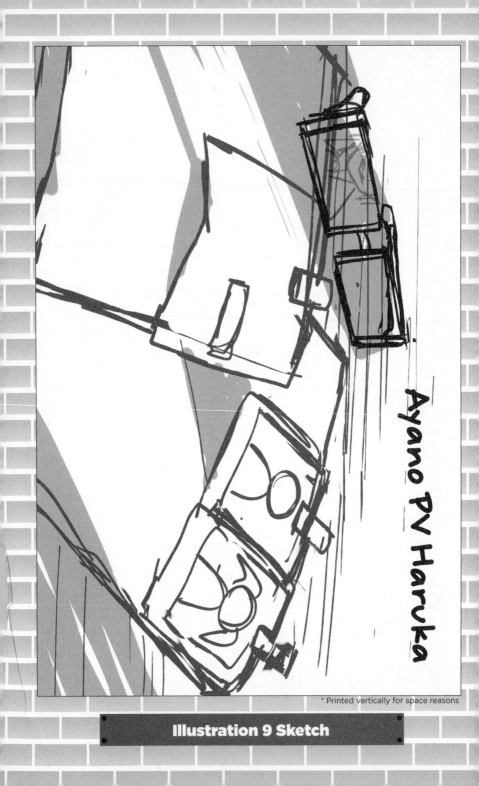

Ayano PV Haruka

* Printed vertically for space reasons

Illustration 9 Sketch

* Printed vertically for space reasons

Illustration 10 Sketch